THE MAN AT THE CORRAL TOOK A STEP TO-
ward his mount, the right side of his body away from
Womack. Then both of them wheeled, drawing guns
as they turned, swiftly and with no words passing
between them, a treacherous act, Womack guessed,
which had been carefully rehearsed and had probably
worked successfully many times.

But Womack was not caught by the Piersons' move.
He drew, a motion which made the Piersons' draw
seem pathetically slow. He fired once, a great sound in
the tight silence, and swung his gun toward Lud
Pierson. He said, "Hold it."

Pierson had his Colt half drawn. He froze that way,
a big comical figure, the bravado gone from him. Joe
had fallen against the corral, struggled to hold himself
upright, and failing, spilled sideways into the litter of
the barnyard.

"Put your iron up, Pierson," Womack said.

Pierson obeyed, Butch crowing: "So you'll kick
folks around, will you, Lud? Maybe that'll learn you.
Didn't even see Wo... ...rst he
didn't have his g... ...thing
I ever seen."

Other *Leisure Books*
by Wayne D. Overholser:

WEST OF THE RIMROCK
DRAW OR DRAG
VALLEY OF GUNS
CAST A LONG SHADOW

WAYNE D. OVERHOLSER

FABULOUS GUNMAN

LEISURE BOOKS ⊔ NEW YORK CITY

To NORMAN A. FOX

**A good writer
And a good friend**

A LEISURE BOOK ®

September 1991

This edition is reprinted by arrangement with MACMILLAN PUBLISHING COMPANY, a division of Macmillan Inc.

Published by
Dorchester Publishing Co., Inc.
276 Fifth Avenue
New York, NY 10001

For further information, contact: Macmillan Publishing Co., a division of Macmillan Inc., 866 Third Avenue, New York, NY 10022

WAYNE D. OVERHOLSER

FABULOUS GUNMAN

Chapter 1: The Job

IT WAS NOT CLEAR IN BILL WOMACK'S MIND WHETHER circumstances had made him what he was, or whether he had given conscious direction to his life. Actually, it made little difference. He was a gunman, no more and no less; an automaton, a killing machine who could be hired; a man graced by nature with speed and muscular rhythm and the kind of patience that permits countless hours of diligent practice.

At twenty-seven Bill Womack had become one of the best, with a reputation that few men attain at twice his age. He had reached the place where he didn't have to look for jobs; jobs looked for him. There had been a time when he would have said this was exactly what he wanted. Now he knew better.

The discontent which had become a canker in Womack was not a new thing; his acute awareness of it was. At the moment he was out of a job and idling away a week in Denver. He had seen a show at the Tabor Grand; he had done some drinking, which was unusual with him; and he had sat in on a poker game until dawn, with his luck running high. He had sucked in on Soapy Smith's game just for the hell of it, amused by the con man's skill with his fingers; but now he was ready to move on. Somewhere. Anywhere.

It was dusk when he came into the lobby of his hotel and stopped at the desk for his key. The clerk looked up, recognized him, and spoke with a forced friendliness that irritated Womack, for it was the way most people treated him when they knew who he was. Because they were afraid of him, they were unduly cordial, as if to assure him they wanted no trouble. Well, he didn't want any trouble, either; but they never thought of that.

The clerk passed his key across the desk. He said, "There's a man looking for you, Mr. Womack, but I didn't know where you were or when you'd be back."

"Who was he?"

"Why, he didn't say, Mr. Womack. He didn't say what he wanted, either. Quite a young fellow. A cowboy, I'd judge, from his clothes."

"I'll be in my room this evening. I'm leaving early in the morning."

"I'm sorry to hear that," the clerk said, as if it were a matter of deep regret. "I hope you have enjoyed your stay with us."

Irritation grew in Womack. The clerk wasn't fooling him: for all of his talk, he just didn't give a damn. "Sure," Womack said, and taking his key, went up the stairs to his room.

Womack lifted his war bag to his bed, took his gun, and slipped it into his waistband. He had not carried a gun since he had come to Denver. There had been little need of it, for no one knew him except the hotel clerks who had recognized his name. It was the first time in months that he had been able to relax the tension which had become habitual with him; but he could not relax now. Not with a man looking for him.

For a long time Womack stood at the window, staring down into the street. He heard the clang of streetcars and the clatter of horses' hoofs on the pavement; he saw street lights and hurrying people, and he wondered where they were going and what bonds held them.

It was idle thinking, for it made no difference to him. He had seen more people this week than he had ever seen in his life before, and he would not change places with any of them. A city was not for him. Still, some of them must be happy, and he could envy them. Not their way of life, the hours at a desk, the pale faces that marked their indoor living, the subdued spirits which enabled them to take another man's orders; but he could envy them their wives and children and homes, their relationship with other men who had no reason to fear them.

He rolled a smoke, smiling a little in self-derision. Those things were not for him, either; not for Bill Womack, who lived by the gun, who never knew whether his next breath would be his last. He could not ask a woman to marry him and face the daily prospect of becoming a widow; he could not father children who might be left orphans at any time.

Womack finished his cigarette and rubbed it out, unconsciously listening for the knock that he knew would come, as he idly considered the reasons that the cowboy might have for wanting to see him. There were the wild ones who wanted to kill him and make themselves a reputation; there were those who had been friends of men he had killed and who wanted to get square; and there were others, attracted by the glitter of his fame, who wanted to throw in with him.

Then he heard the steps in the hall and the tap on his door. Shrugging, he crossed the room. This was an old experience in small cow towns where his name had become a legend, but he had not expected it to happen here where he had hoped to lose himself

among the thousands. As he opened the door, a
vagrant regret touched him. He wished he had signed
the hotel register as John Smith.

The man who stood there was young, perhaps under
twenty, with the gangling immaturity of youth still
upon him. He seemed to sprout up out of his boots as
leggy as a young colt; his neck was long, his wind-
burned face thin and bony. Dark eyes met Womack's
pale blue ones squarely, and there was nothing of the
brash showiness about him that marked most kids
who were trying to fill boots that were too big for
them.

"You Bill Womack?"

"I'm Womack."

"If you ain't too busy, I'd like to talk to you."

Womack stepped aside. "Come in."

"I'm Ed Hovey." He held out his hand. "From
Dillon Mesa on the western slope."

Womack shook hands, liking young Hovey's grip;
he was thinking that here was a boy who had no past
to plague him, no reputation to defend. There were
thousands like him, skilled with rope and iron, knowing a good horse as soon as they saw one, capable of
holding up their end at roundup, accepted as men on
the home range. Again Womack felt the tug of envy.
He would have been like that if he could have lived his
life over.

For a long moment Hovey stood staring at Womack,
eyes moving from the hair that was as light as oat
straw on down the slender medium-tall body to the
new, expensive boots which he had bought the first
day he'd been in Denver. Hovey's eyes swung upward,
paused briefly on the black-butted .44 in Womack's
waistband, and lifted to meet his gaze.

"You don't look nothing like I figured," Hovey said.

Womack smiled and motioned to the one chair that
was in the room. "Sit down." He dropped to the bed
and leaned back. "What'd you expect to see?"

"I dunno." Hovey took the chair and sat there awkwardly, his hands on his knees. "Somebody that was full of hell and vinegar, I guess. I never seen a real gun slinger before. We've got some tough hands on our range, like the Pierson boys; at least they act tough. You know, shove folks around so nobody'll forget they're wanted in three states."

"I ain't wanted by the law," Womack said.

"I know," Hovey said quickly. "That's why I'm here. I meant—well, everybody who ever heard of you knows what you've done and can do. I guess you ain't afraid of nothing, and they say you're hell on high red wheels with your six; but you look, well, just like common folks."

It pleased Womack. There were times when he thought he must look like hell on high red wheels, judging by the way folks treated him. He said: "Don't let nobody fool you about me not being afraid. Them that say they ain't are just damn' fool liars." He reached for the makings and rolled a smoke, looking down at the tobacco and paper. "And I've noticed that the fellows who want everybody to think they're tough usually ain't got the bottom it takes when it comes to cases."

"I reckon it's that way with the Piersons," Hovey admitted.

"What'd you want to see me about?"

Hovey looked down at his toes. "I wanted to give you a job, but now that I've seen you—" He stopped, embarrassed. "I don't mean that the way it sounded. It's just that you don't look like a man who'd take a job without knowing all there is to know about it."

Five minutes ago Womack would have said Hovey was right, that he was done with anything that even smelled like gunpowder. He was leaving in the morning, and he had aimed to follow his nose for a while. Instead he said, "I'll listen."

Hovey scratched the floor with his boot toe, still not

looking up. "We live on Dillon Mesa. That's over the divide from Montrose. Cow country. You've run into the same thing a dozen times, I reckon. Four big outfits and some little ten-cow spreads and a few farmers below town. Dogdance—that's the name of the burg—has got some businessmen who suck around after the big gun. He's Cole Chapman. He don't act tough, neither, but he's got a way of running things."

"What's the job?"

"I don't rightly know." Hovey looked up, red creeping into his face. "This sounds loco, but I figure you'll find out after you get there." He lifted a wallet from his coat pocket and tossed it on the bed. "There's $1,000 and a ticket to Colatas. That's the nearest station on the narrow gauge to Dogdance. You can take a train out tonight. You'll change at Montrose, then, after you get to Colatas, you ride the stage to Dogdance."

"You're damned sure I'd take the job," Womack said, irritated by Hovey's certainty.

"I was till I saw you. Now I'm just hoping you will. There's another thing. When you get to Dogdance, keep mum and see how things shape up. They'll be having a meeting of the combine 'bout the time you get there. That's the owners of the four big outfits. My dad's one of 'em. You walk in and say Chapman sent for you."

"Why, I'd be—"

"Yeah, I reckon you would, but it's got to be that way. I've got a twin sister named Rose. She'll see you after you get to Dogdance and give you another thousand."

Womack got up and walked to the window. He had been offered some queer deals, but nothing like this before. Still, he was stirred by curiosity. Furthermore, he liked the boy, and he sensed a need for help that young Hovey had not put into words. He looked down into the street, the thought entering his mind that perhaps the discontent which had been mounting in him came from being in a city. He had to get out, and $2,000 was not to be taken lightly.

"How'd you know I was here?"

"Rose saw it in the *Rocky Mountain News* just before I left Montrose. I came to Denver to buy some Hereford bulls. Rose 'n' me have got a herd of our own. It's our money we're paying you with. Rose said for me to see you. The paper just said you was registered here."

Womack put his back to the window. Hovey was looking at him, waiting expectantly. To gain a little time to think, Womack asked, "Got white faces on your range?"

"Naw. Just scrub stuff. Can't talk Chapman into buying good stock. Says it ain't worth it, but me 'n' Rose figure it is."

Womack stood looking at the boy, seeing the trouble in his dark eyes. He said: "I just walk in. Play it the way I see it. No orders. No nothing."

Hovey ran a hand across his face. "I don't know what's up. They'll be deciding what to do the next time the combine meets. I don't trust Chapman. That's the one thing I am sure about. He's got Dad wrapped up and tied. That's what we want you to do mostly. Keep Dad out of trouble. You've got to know him and Chapman before you savvy just how it is."

"Why do I say Chapman hired me?"

"Rose 'n' me don't want Dad to know we're fetching you to the mesa. It'll work, all right. Chapman's bent on running everybody out but the combine, but me 'n' Rose don't see no sense to it." He pinned defiant eyes on Womack. "Anyhow, me 'n' Rose want you working for us, not Chapman. We figure that'll make some difference in what you do."

"Yeah, I reckon it would," Womack said softly. "Maybe Chapman was talking about sending for me."

"Maybe he was," Hovey admitted.

"Strikes me that this job is to stop trouble. Usually, when anybody hires me, it's to make trouble."

"Sure," Hovey said hotly, "and most gun slingers don't give a damn who they work for or what the trouble's over. I didn't figure you was that way. If you are, don't take the job."

Womack had been exactly like most gun slingers. He had no illusions about his morals or his conscience, and he had never been one to judge the men he worked for. Now, entirely honest with himself, he realized that the sourness which had grown in him through this week went back much farther into the past. It was not just being in a city. If a man cut away from his past, he had to cut sharply and at once. This might be the way.

Womack said, "I'll take that train, Hovey."

That night, lying in a lower berth, the steady *clickety-click* of wheels on rails beat against his ears, and he could not sleep. Suddenly, and for the first time in his life, the ghosts of the men who had died before his gun crowded around him, pointing at him and laughing derisively and shouting, "You've gone soft, Womack, as soft as mush on a nester's stove."

He sat up, striking at them and crying out, and then realized he had been asleep. He lay back, shame working through him, and he wondered why the ghosts in his dream had said, "As soft as mush on a *nester's* stove." Then he knew, for he was remembering the last man he had killed. A farmer who had stood in front of his soddy in western Nebraska. Sure, it had been a fair fight. (He had justified himself that way.) The farmer had gone for his gun. But it was a hell of a poor excuse, for the farmer had had no chance against Bill Womack.

It was not in him to regret for long the things that had been done, for no amount of regret could undo them. The past was a long kinked rope running back to his boyhood years. He thought again that if he was to escape from it, he must cut it with one quick stroke; and this job for young Ed Hovey and his twin sister Rose might be the way. With that thought, Bill Womack went to sleep.

Chapter 2: Duel at Moran's

COLATAS WAS A PINPRICK ON THE MAP; IT WAS LITTLE MORE than that on the narrow gauge. Womack stood beside the depot as the little train snorted and clattered eastward up Devil River toward the big mining camps in the San Juan range, his eyes on the settlement. There were a store, a few scattered houses, and some shipping pens on down the track. That was all.

This was new country to Womack. He knew eastern Colorado well. He had even picked out a little ranch in South Park that he wanted to own someday, but his bank account in Cheyenne had never reached the figure which would enable him to go out and buy what he wanted.

He liked what he had seen of the western slope: the Gunnison country, the Uncompahgre Valley around Montrose, the magnificent Sneffels range that he had seen from the car window as the train crossed Dallas summit. Now he looked up at the canyon walls which crowded in against Devil River, marked here and there by streaks of red rock and patches of aspen that were already beginning to turn orange, then he brought his eyes to the river that rushed by as if it were in a hurry to reach the Dolores. It would be a good fishing stream, he thought, if the big mills upstream had not dumped their tailings into it.

He had been only vaguely aware of the girl who was standing in the shadow of the depot, her eyes on him.

Now she moved toward him, asking, "Are you Bill Womack?"

He turned, his hand touching his hat brim. "I'm Womack."

The girl smiled, as if relieved. "I'm awfully glad to see you, Mr. Womack." She held out her hand. "I'm Rose Hovey."

He gripped her hand, liking the firm clasp that she gave him. "Your brother said you'd see me in Dogdance. I wasn't expecting you here."

"I thought I'd wait on my way home from Montrose," she said. "I didn't really expect you, but I kept hoping."

She was pretty. That was his first thought. Her features were well shaped, she had a strong chin, her eyes were dark blue, and her hair was a sort of brownish-red. Auburn, he guessed, would be the word. She was quite small, not much over five feet tall, and shapely enough in her tan waist and brown riding skirt. Then he thought "pretty" didn't say it. Not about Rose Hovey, for he sensed an honest dignity and strength in her that he felt in few women, and it brought an instant respect from him.

He was silent for a time, searching for the proper words. At that moment it seemed important to get off on the right foot with her. He said haltingly: "I wasn't sure I should come. Your brother didn't give me much to go on."

"He couldn't," she said quickly. "I can't, either. It's like sitting on a keg of powder that somebody has lighted a fuse to, and you can't find the fuse."

"You want me to find it and yank it out? That it?"

"That's exactly it. Ed probably told you that I'd have another thousand dollars for you. I'll get it out of the bank as soon as we get to Dogdance."

"Better wait till I find that fuse," he said.

She smiled, liking that. "All right, if you want it that way." She heard the rattle of the stage and turned from him. "I guess Butch is ready to roll."

The stage wheeled up and stopped, the driver calling, "Hop in."

Womack grinned when he saw the driver. The name Butch didn't fit. He was a small man with a leather-brown face, a bulging chew of tobacco in one cheek, and a wispy mustache that didn't quite achieve what its owner hoped it would.

Womack gave Rose a hand and tossed his war bag inside, wondering why he was noticing things he ordinarily would have paid no attention to. He stepped in and shut the door. Butch let out the silk, and with the pistol-sharp crack the horses started at a brisk pace.

The girl sat beside Womack on the back seat, her head turned so that she could look at him. She had no shame about it; she was studying him as coolly as a horse buyer would size up an animal he was about to purchase. Womack felt a touch of irritation, then it passed, and he grinned. There was some humor in this. She was a little late looking him over. He had already been bought.

"You know," Womack said, "you've got freckles on your nose."

"I'm ashamed of myself for staring at you like that." She frowned and looked away. "You just don't look like the man I'd pictured as Bill Womack."

"Your brother said the same thing. He figured I'd look like I was full of hell and vinegar."

She laughed. "That sounds like Ed. I guess I had the same notion, but you're like any cowhand except for the way you carry your gun. And you're younger than I thought you'd be."

"It ain't the years," he said. "It's what happens to you during them years."

"That's right, of course. What did Ed tell you?"

He told her, adding: "It ain't much. I need to know more'n that if I'm going to earn my wages."

"Just find the fuse," she said gravely. "It's on account of Dad we sent for you. He—well, he drinks

too much. Something's happened to him. I don't
know what. Maybe it's just disappointment. He was
the first one on Dillon Mesa. Ed and I were children
when he drove a herd over the mountains. He had his
pick of locations, and he made the wrong choice."

Womack didn't like the sound of it. He respected
strength, but too often the men who hired him were
like this Hovey. They had money and they were
respectable; they belonged to the local cattlemen's
association; they probably belonged to the local lodge,
and they were looked up to; while men like Bill
Womack, who ironed out their troubles, were given
the kind of grudging respect that was rooted in fear, or
even hate.

Rose was silent for a time. Then she said: "The rest
of them came later. Abner Lowrie's Slash Triangle is
up near the head of Ute Creek. Red Manion—he's the
sheriff—started his Mallet Four between us and
Lowrie's place. Chapman was the last to come, and he
was the smartest of all of them. His CC outfit is just
five miles east of Dogdance, and he's right out in the
middle of the mesa, with the best winter graze in the
country."

"What about water?"

"There's plenty. The main stream is Ute Creek,
which goes into Devil River six or seven miles below
Dogdance, but there are a lot of little creeks that come
out of the mountains and flow all summer." She made
a small gesture as if to dismiss the subject. "Chapman
is the one who's made a fortune, and he's got Dad and
the others lined up so they'll do what he wants.
Chapman is the kind who has all he needs and then
some; but he wants everything, so he's trying to drive
the little fellows out of the country."

It was an old, familiar pattern to Womack. It was
often that way with a man who had established
himself as a local leader. Success seemed to hold the
seeds of greed; and more often than not the county law
was a pliant force that was controlled by the greedy

ones. Here was another weakness in human nature that went against Womack's grain. People would bow and scrape in front of the man who paid for the killings, but the one who pulled the trigger was considered a pariah.

There was another run of silence while the stage wheeled downstream beside the plunging river. Then Rose said: "Chapman has formed what he calls the combine. If he was in this just by himself, he'd have trouble and people would blame him, but as long as he can speak for the combine he gives the feeling that all the big cowmen are behind him."

"Looks like this is too big a job for me," Womack said. "Your brother told me to act like I was working for Chapman, but there ain't much I can do if he gives the orders."

She gave him a searching look. "Do you always take orders?"

He shrugged. "I hire my gun. My job is usually to do what I'm told."

"What about the law? And justice?"

Law! Justice! They were words he had not thought much about. To some they meant the same things, but often they meant the opposite. In cases like this, the law usually bolstered the power of those who held the reins, and justice was not a consideration.

"I don't know," Womack said after a time. "I guess it depends on the way you see things."

She shook her head. "No matter how you see things, there's no justice in driving a rancher off his place because he lacks the money to hire gun fighters. I know Dad doesn't think there is. When he's sober he hates Chapman. He just won't stand against him."

"You expect me to give him courage?"

She spread her hands. "I don't know what you can do. That's why Ed couldn't tell any more than he did. I can't, either."

He stared unseeingly at the cliff that lifted at the edge of the road, and he thought, just as he had when he'd talked to Ed Hovey, that this was the queerest job he'd ever taken. In other jobs his orders had given him no chance to consider justice. You moved a man off a piece of land that someone else wanted, or away from a waterhole or into a deal that half robbed him. He did what you said or you killed him; then you collected your money and left. But this was different, and somehow he liked it.

"I'll do what I can," he said, "but I may need advice."

She smiled, as if relieved. "I'm long on giving advice. Trouble is, most men don't take it."

He could have said he'd take her advice because he was paid to take it, but he didn't voice the words. He was looking at the cliff again, at the boulders and the cedars that found precarious footing there, and he felt the challenge that this girl and her brother were giving him. He was to prevent trouble, not make it; to bring justice where there was no justice, to save a man from his own weakness.

The valley suddenly widened, and an alfalfa field lay between the road and the river. The stage turned sharply to the left, and the driver pulled to a stop with a flourish in front of a farmhouse, calling out, "Got the grub on the table, Moran?"

"It's on and hot," a man called back. "What's the matter, Butch? You're three minutes late."

"The hell I am," the driver said indignantly. "Your clock's off. Must be the same kind of time the railroad uses. The train was five minutes late getting into Colatas."

Womack stepped down and gave Rose a hand. She stretched and yawned and shook her head. "I don't care much for stages. I thought of getting horses, but I didn't know how you'd like that, and I wanted to talk to you."

"And you didn't know I'd come."

"No," she said. "I didn't."

The farmer motioned to his log house. "It's on the table, ma'am. Fifteen minutes to eat."

Womack followed Rose inside, and a moment later the driver came in, still complaining about Moran saying he was three minutes late. It was a good meal of steak and biscuits and vegetables from Moran's garden, a better meal than Womack was used to at stage stops. He ate hungrily and gulped a second cup of steaming coffee when he saw Butch get up.

The driver walked to the door. He stopped there, suddenly tense as a man demanded arrogantly, "Who've you got on the stage, Butch?"

Rose gripped Womack's arm. "It's Lud Pierson."

Womack remembered that Ed Hovey had mentioned the tough Pierson boys; he saw that Rose was trembling. Butch was saying, "Just two passengers, Lud: Rose Hovey and a stranger who came in on the train."

"I'll have a look at that stranger," the arrogant voice said.

Womack pushed Butch aside and went out into the sunlight. "Take your look, friend."

Lud Pierson was big and showy in his pearl-colored Stetson and calfskin vest and green silk shirt with Mexican coins instead of buttons. His gold-plated Colt was cased in an elaborate holster; his big-roweled spurs were silver. Now he stared at Womack, his heavy features squeezed into a scowl.

"A gun fighter, are you?" Pierson demanded.

"Some call me that," Womack said.

It was then that Womack saw the second man who was standing motionless beside the corral. He looked much like Lud Pierson except that he was smaller and younger and not so showy. A brother, Womack guessed, and probably the better fighting man of the two. Womack always associated showy clothes and a belligerent manner with an inner weakness; they were usually assumed to cover that weakness.

"You're working for Cole Chapman?" Pierson asked.

"Maybe."

"Well, don't take the stage to Dogdance. Chapman's been putting out some talk about sending for a pack of gun wolves, but we ain't standing for it. Savvy?"

"Who's we?"

"All of us on Dillon Mesa who don't belong to the combine. We've got our places and we aim to keep 'em, by hell. We ain't gonna be bluffed by no damned drifter just because he totes a gun."

"I figured I'd go to Dogdance," Womack said, his voice mild.

"Well, I'm figuring different." Pierson motioned to the driver. "Get rolling, Butch. Rose, tell your pa and Chapman that this don't go. Let 'em come after us if they want to run us out of the country, and we'll let 'em have more hot lead than they ever seen."

Womack said nothing while Butch crossed the yard and climbed to the high seat. Rose stood in the doorway, waiting. Butch said, "Come on, Rose."

Womack walked toward the stage, covertly watching the man at the corral. Pierson bawled, "Now where the hell do you think you're going, mister?"

"I said I figured I'd go to Dogdance," Womack answered, his voice still mild.

"No you ain't. If I didn't make myself clear, I'll be damned sure I do now. You stay here at Moran's till Butch makes his trip back to Colatas. Then you get on the stage and get to hell out of the country. Now do you savvy?"

"You don't know who you're talking to, Lud," Rose cried. "This is Bill Womack."

"Womack." It was Butch in the high seat, echoing the word.

The swagger drained out of Lud Pierson. Suddenly he seemed to be smaller, his red face not so red now. He said, his tone overly friendly: "So you're the great

Womack. Chapman hired the best, just like he said he
would."

"Some say I'm the best," Womack admitted. "You
still figure on me staying here?"

"Why, no. I didn't know who you were." Pierson
turned toward his horse, adding: "Come on, Joe. Let's
ride."

The man at the corral took a step toward his mount,
the right side of his body away from Womack. Then
both of them wheeled, drawing guns as they turned,
swiftly and with no words passing between them, a
treacherous act, Womack guessed, which had been
carefully rehearsed and had probably worked successfully many times.

But Womack was not caught by the Piersons' move.
He drew, a motion which made the Piersons' draw
seem pathetically slow. He fired once, a great sound in
the tight silence, and swung his gun toward Lud
Pierson. He said, "Hold it."

Pierson had his Colt half drawn. He froze that way,
a big comical figure, the bravado gone from him. Joe
had fallen against the corral, struggled to hold himself
upright, and failing, spilled sideways into the litter of
the barnyard.

"Put your iron up, Pierson," Womack said.

Pierson obeyed, Butch crowing: "So you'll kick
folks around, will you, Lud? Maybe that'll learn you.
Didn't even see Womack draw, did you? First he
didn't have his gun and then he did. Damnedest thing
I ever seen."

"Load your man on your horse and git," Womack
ordered.

They remained motionless, Butch in the high seat,
Rose in the doorway, Moran over by the barn door,
and Womack in the middle of the yard, his gun in his
hand. None of them moved until Pierson had finished
tying Joe into the saddle. He mounted and rode away,
not looking back.

Womack said, "Reckon we can go now."

Rose walked past him to the stage. He opened the door and gave her a hand, then climbed in beside her, and the stage rolled. Neither spoke until the coach had wheeled across the bridge and started up the long twisting grade that led to the top of the south canyon wall. Then Rose said, "You're all they say you are, Mr. Womack."

He rolled a cigarette, not knowing what to say. Finally he asked, "Them two brothers?"

She nodded. "Outlaws. The sheriff knows that, but they've been careful not to get into trouble in Colorado, so Manion doesn't bother them. Their sister Molly has a little farm on Ute Creek where they live part of the time. When they aren't there, they stay in an outlaw hideout across the river called Owl's Hole. Molly sells food to anybody who hides out there for a while."

"Why did they jump me?" Womack asked.

"I don't know," she answered slowly, "unless Ira Slade sent them to watch the stage. He's the leader of the little ranchers, and they know they're going to have to fight or get out."

Womack fired his cigarette, broke the match and threw it out of the window. He felt no regret about the killing. The Piersons had been treacherous; they would have killed him if they could. Then he glanced at the girl's tight face and wished it hadn't happened. Rose Hovey had not wanted trouble; she had hired him to prevent it, and now he had killed a man before he had even reached Dogdance. He wanted respect from her, not fear.

"I'm sorry I had to do that," he said at last, "but they'd have ventilated me proper if I hadn't."

"Of course," she said quickly. "No one will blame you. Everybody's been afraid of the Piersons for years, and that includes the sheriff."

"Maybe this has shaped up more'n you figure," he said. "Maybe it's got to the place where nothing I can do will stop the fireworks."

Rose gave him a searching look. "Perhaps, but I hope you'll try." She took a long breath. "Mr. Womack, I've been thinking about what you said a while ago. About taking orders and hiring your gun and about justice."

She stopped and looked away, apparently uncertain what to say; and because it seemed important to have her respect, Womack asked in a low voice, "What were you thinking?"

She brought her eyes to him, almost defiantly. "I'll tell you. If you use your talent because someone orders you to kill a man, and if you don't give the justice of it any thought, you're a traitor to God and man."

He looked down at the river that was a small ribbon below them. Butch had stopped to let the horses blow. There was this moment of silence with just a whisper of the wind among the cedars. Something that had started a long time ago and had come to a head in Denver now crystallized in him.

"Looks like I'll have to do some thinking," he said. "About justice."

Chapter 3: The Combine

WOMACK HAD NEVER SEEN A COUNTRY LIKE THIS. DILLON Mesa was a great grass-covered plain with a series of benches to the south, laid one upon another to form a long dark line against a brilliant sky. There was only one break, a conelike peak that stood alone in the middle of the line, bare granite lifting above timber line without a trace of snow.

The San Juan range made jagged saw teeth to the east, and westward the La Sals pricked the horizon.

Between the road and the La Sals the flat dropped off
into a maze of dark canyons, a broken country that
from Dillon Mesa seemed to be impenetrable. To the
north, across Devil River, another ridge, spruce-
covered, humped up against the sky. Over there
somewhere would be the Owl's Hole that Rose had
mentioned.

The stage ran on, the sun in the western sky beating
across it with stifling heat. Dust rose from hoofs and
wheels and drifted into the coach, making the girl
cover her face with a handkerchief. Womack said
nothing until they were almost in Dogdance. Then he
asked, "What do you call that mountain south of
here?"

Rose lowered her handkerchief. "Angel Peak. When
the snow comes, it forms a figure on this side that
looks like an angel. West of it is a wall you can't see
from here. It's several hundred feet high and straight
up, so we call it Hell's Wall."

"Devil River. Hell's Wall. Angel Peak." He grinned.
"Some country."

"Some country," she agreed. "My mother died
before we came here, but I remember the way she used
to talk to Ed and me about right and wrong and God
and the devil. Since we came here, I've thought about
it a lot. Seems like the old timers who gave names to
everything around here have been thinking about the
same things."

"I reckon," he said, and let it go at that.

Rose put her handkerchief back to her face. They
were silent until they reached the first house that
marked the edge of Dogdance. Then she wadded up
the handkerchief and slipped it into her pocket. She
said: "They'll probably be having a meeting of the
combine in the Starlight. If they are, you'd better
attend. The sooner you meet Chapman, the better."

Womack grinned at her. "Won't he be surprised
when I tell him he sent for me."

"You won't know it if he is," she said. "Nothing ever seems to surprise him." She paused, then added, "Unless it's some of the things his wife Nita does."

There was more she wanted to tell him, Womack thought, but she didn't offer to go on and he didn't press her. There were some things he'd have to find out for himself. Rose, he was sure, was not a person to say anything against anyone else unless she was certain.

The stage wheeled between two rows of false fronts and stopped before the hotel. Womack stepped down and gave Rose a hand. Then he moved to the walk and had a look at Dogdance. He saw at once that it might have been any of a dozen cow towns where he had tarried: one short block with a wide rutted street, the red dust hock-deep; broken boards in the walk, gnawed hitching rails, and the usual business places, including three saloons, two general stores, a bank, a livery stable, a blacksmith shop, and a building with the faded words DOGDANCE HOTEL written across its false front. There were a few dogs sleeping in the sun and some children playing marbles at the end of the block, and over all there hung a sleepy air that was as deceptive as the quiet before a thunderstorm.

From where Womack stood he could see the Starlight, the most pretentious saloon in town and probably the one favored by the men who rode for the combine. There were two other saloons at opposite ends of the block; and if this town followed the usual pattern, one would cater to the small cowmen, the other to the farmers.

A crowd had moved up to see who was on the stage. Several people spoke to Rose, asking where she had been, wanting to know what was going on in Montrose and whether there was any news about the gold camps up Devil River. Womack picked up his war bag and went into the hotel.

"I'll leave my war sack here," Womack said as he

signed the register. "I've got some business that won't wait."

"Sure." The clerk nodded and spun the register. He saw the name and raised startled eyes to Womack. "You—you ain't the Bill Womack we hear about?"

"Dunno about that, but I'm Womack."

Womack walked out, the clerk's eyes following him. Rose was still standing in front of the hotel, talking, and as Womack passed she called, "Mr. Womack, I want you to meet Mrs. Chapman."

He stopped, his eyes held by the beauty of the tall dark woman who stood beside Rose. She said, "I was envious when Rose said she'd ridden all the way from Colatas with the famous Bill Womack. Welcome to Dogdance, Mr. Womack."

He touched the brim of his Stetson, mumbling, "Thank you, Mrs. Chapman," and wondered if every man felt like this the first time he saw Nita Chapman. She was beautiful with a beauty that shocked him, a beauty that sprang from perfection of features and a bright, challenging spirit. Womack wondered how much of Cole Chapman's strength and position on the mesa he owed to his wife.

Womack would have moved on toward the Starlight if Mrs. Chapman had not said: "It isn't often that a celebrity comes to our out-of-the-way town. I want to get acquainted with you before you leave."

"I won't be going right away, ma'am."

"One never knows how long he will be in Dogdance," she said quickly. "I'd like for you to have supper with me. With my husband, too, if he stays in town."

Womack hesitated, his gaze swinging to Rose Hovey's face, and he thought she was frowning. Something lay behind the fixed smile on her lips, as if her thoughts had turned back to their hours together on the stage; but whatever it was, she dismissed it and said easily, "Mrs. Chapman is a charming hostess."

"I—I may be busy tonight," Womack said.

"Not your first evening in town," Mrs. Chapman said, as if it were unthinkable. "What kind of busy work?"

"I don't know yet. I'll have to find out."

Womack touched his hat brim again and walked away. The slight frown had returned to Rose's face, and he wondered if she was wishing she had told him more about Nita Chapman. Perhaps she had held back because she was not sure of herself; but Nita was the kind who could be the storm center on Dillon Mesa, and Womack doubted if anyone knew what went on in her head. Rose was honest and utterly lacking in subterfuge; Nita Chapman would be the opposite in every way. Womack was never certain in his judgments of women; he had learned to read most men, but he instinctively distrusted beautiful women.

Womack pushed through the batwings and went into the Starlight. It was not a big saloon, but it was expensively furnished with an ornate mahogany bar and a glittering chandelier, and three poker tables were ranged along the east wall. A huge painting of a scantily clad woman reclining on a couch hung above the middle poker table. It was the sort of saloon Womack would expect to find in a mining camp, but it seemed as out of place in Dogdance as Nita Chapman had.

When Womack came up to the bar, the apron asked, "What'll it be, mister?"

"Where's the combine meeting?"

The barman put fat hands down upon the polished mahogany and leaned forward, amusement touching his soft face. "Now what would that be to you, mister?"

There was only one other man in the saloon. He rose from the poker table where he had been playing solitaire and came toward Womack, asking, "He wants to see the big fellows, does he, Alec?"

The barman nodded. "Maybe he's got a gun for hire."

"Now maybe he has." The solitaire player held out his hand. "I'm Black Garrity, friend. Sort of a watchdog, you might say, for Cole Chapman."

Womack gripped the soft, long-fingered hand, then dropped it with an instinctive aversion. He always felt that way when he gripped a hand as soft as this one of Garrity's. The man was small and swarthy, his eyes black and piercing and unreadable. A professional gambler, Womack judged. Probably fast with the gun he carried in a shoulder holster under his Prince Albert, and probably hand in glove with Cole Chapman. For some reason Womack thought of Nita Chapman, and wondered how she'd make out playing poker with this Black Garrity.

"Funny," Womack murmured. "I had a notion that Cole Chapman wouldn't be needing a watchdog."

Garrity laughed softly. "A man never gets so big he doesn't need a watchdog. Not a barker but a good biter."

"That may be," Womack agreed. "A man can get pretty big if he has enough biters on his payroll."

Garrity nodded, still smiling. "But he's got to know about the biters. Some of them might sharpen their teeth on him. Now Cole is a smart hombre, mister, very smart. With him a man could go a long ways on this range. If he's against him . . ." Garrity shrugged. "Well, you'll find out if you're with Ira Slade."

"I ain't. I'm Bill Womack."

The smile died on Garrity's thin lips. The barman gave out a gusty breath, whispering, "Womack," as if lacking the strength to say the word any louder.

"You were a long time getting around to that, friend." Garrity jerked his head at a door in the rear of the room. "Back yonder. Go on in."

"Thanks."

Womack swung around and took two steps before Garrity asked: "Are you as good as they say, friend?

Or maybe lucky? Or just riding the publicity you've had?"

"I'm good," Womack said, and went on along the bar, leaving Garrity staring speculatively after him.

Womack didn't knock. He opened the door, went in, and closed it behind him. He stood there, taking a quick look at the four men in the room. The pudgy one with the purple-veined face would be Grant Hovey. The big fellow with the star would be Red Manion. Womack wasn't sure about the other two. One was close to thirty, lean and hawk-nosed; the other was older, a small man who sat with his chair canted back against the wall, a long cigar cocked between his molars. He brought the front legs of his chair down against the floor and leaned forward, blinking at Womack from behind the thick lenses of his glasses.

"You've got gall, friend," the small man said, "butting in without bothering to knock."

"You need gall in my business," Womack said. "Which one of you is Cole Chapman?"

"I am," the small man said.

Womack did not let his face show surprise. He had guessed wrong, for he'd pegged the hawk-nosed one as Chapman. Womack said: "I'm Bill Womack. I got here as soon as I could."

"Womack," Hovey breathed. "Now what the hell are you doing here?"

"Ask Chapman," Womack answered.

Chapman chewed on his cigar, his round little face inscrutable, his eyes impossible to read behind the heavy glasses. He said, "You must have wings, Womack."

"No. Gunmen don't have wings." Womack grinned a little. "It seemed like a good job, so I moved along. Just got in on the stage."

Chapman rose as if he had come to a decision. "Meeting's over. No use fetching our boys down from Angel Peak now that we've got Womack. No use sitting around while Slade and his bunch starve out. If Womack is as good as he's supposed to be, he'll get this job done in a hurry."

Red Manion got up and shoved his big hands into his pants pockets. "I don't like it, Cole. I'm supposed to be the law. What happens when this gun thrower goes to work?"

"We'll have some burying to do," Chapman said crisply. "This Womack don't look tough, but a man don't get his reputation just by using a bean shooter."

"That's right," Womack murmured. "I never use a bean shooter."

"What'n hell am I supposed to do?" Manion demanded. "Go fishing?"

"Good idea," Chapman said. "Now get out of here. I want to talk to Womack."

"I won't stand for it," Manion said doggedly. "I'll play along for a while, but damn it—"

"You'll play along, all right," Chapman cut in. "You like that star, don't you?"

"Come on, Red," Hovey said. "If Cole says it's all right, it's all right."

Hovey moved toward the door. The hawk-nosed man rose and crossed the room to stand beside Hovey, but Manion remained motionless, glowering. He said: "I'll stand for the pushing, Cole. Maybe Slade's bunch has stolen some of our beef. It's all right to move 'em out anyhow. You've tied up their credit with the stores and you've told Paddy Ryan to see that the bank don't loan 'em nothing. They'll freeze out if we wait. Why, hell, with you tying up the mining camps, they ain't got no market." He swung a hand out toward Womack. "But paying this hairpin big money—"

"You've had your say," Chapman bellowed. "Now go fishing. Ride up to Angel Peak and see how the boys are doing. Just get off the mesa. This is one time we don't need a sheriff."

"That's right," Womack said. "I always work better when there ain't a tin star around to ball things up."

"How do we know this fellow's Womack?" Manion demanded. "Looks like a grub-line rider to me."

"There's one way you can find out," Womack said softly.

"Damn you, Red," Chapman said, his voice low. "You've come a long ways playing on my side. If you want to throw in with Ira Slade, say so."

"Come on, Red," Hovey urged. "Let's have a drink."

Reluctantly Manion walked out, Hovey following. The hawk-nosed man stood there a moment, smiling a little, as if the whole thing was amusing. Then he went out and shut the door. He would be the Abner Lowrie whom Rose had mentioned and who owned the Slash Triangle near the head of Ute Creek. He had not said a word, and somehow it bothered Womack. A man usually gave himself away by what he said. Like Hovey, who would back anything Chapman did. And Red Manion, who had taken a stand but wasn't man enough to hold it. But a silent man was hard to peg.

Chapter 4: Nita

WHEN THE DOOR CLOSED, CHAPMAN SAT DOWN AND MO-tioned for Womack to draw up a chair. He said crisply: "Well, Womack, there's something damned funny about this. I didn't send for you, which same you know as well as I do."

Womack dropped into a chair and rolled a smoke. "Heard you wanted a man like me, so I came on. I didn't hear you denying you sent for me."

"I've done some talking," Chapman admitted. "Mentioned you and Doc Holliday and a few others. As a matter of fact, I was bluffing, figuring that Slade and his bunch would cave before it got to the shooting stage. Now that you're here, I reckon the shooting'll start."

"Time for it?" Womack asked.

"Yes, I guess it is," Chapman said slowly, as if reluctant. "I'm giving you just one order. Don't go hog wild. Let it get around that you're here. Might be you won't have to burn any powder."

"I've been in the business a long time," Womack said. "I never go hog wild."

"Sure, sure." Chapman chewed on his cigar, making a cool study of Womack. Then he said: "You don't look like I thought you would. Manion might be right. How do we know you're Womack?"

"How do I know you're Chapman? I had you figured for a man seven feet tall."

Chapman's face reddened. "It ain't how big a man is that counts. It's what he does, and I do plenty. I built the CC into a spread that's bigger'n the Slash Triangle, the Bow and Arrow, and the Mallet Four all rolled into one. I got here last and I went ahead of all of 'em. Abner Lowrie's dad might have held me down, but he's dead. You saw what the three of 'em were. I don't have to be seven feet tall."

"I don't, neither. I was just showing you that a man don't have to look like people think he oughta look. The Pierson boys jumped me at Moran's stage station. Joe's dead and Lud toted his body off. That prove anything?"

Chapman relaxed. "Yeah, it proves plenty. How'd it happen?"

Womack told him, and Chapman said, "Hell, you should 'a' plugged Lud."

"No," Womack said. "Lud will get the word around that I'm here."

Chapman nodded. "I guess that's right. I just don't

like Lud, strutting around like a turkey gobbler with his tail spread." He fished a match out of his pocket and fired his cigar. "How much do you know about this range?"

"Rose Hovey was on the stage. She told me how it was."

Chapman snorted. "Rose and that twin brother of hers are soft. Soft as old Grant himself. Well, what's your fee for this job?"

Womack ground out his cigarette. "I never buy a horse before I give him a try. Suppose we decide after the job's done?"

"You guarantee anything?"

Womack had expected that. Cole Chapman would drive a shrewd bargain on any matter which had to do with money, a side of him that explained how he had attained the position he held on Dillon Mesa.

"I'll guarantee one thing," Womack said. "The range will be cleared."

"That's good enough for me," Chapman said. "Play it your way and leave me out of it. You take the chances and you get paid for it. Savvy?"

Womack nodded. "What kind of a hairpin is this Ira Slade?"

"He ain't much like Lud Pierson. No show. A hard worker. Got a little ten-cow spread 'bout ten miles east of here where the mesa breaks off into a bunch of canyons. He's the kind who won't listen good. You'll have to show him."

Womack rose. "I met your wife when I left the hotel."

Chapman's face softened. "Beautiful, ain't she?" he asked eagerly. "Purtiest woman on the western slope."

"Mighty purty," Womack agreed. "She asked me to have supper with her and you if you was staying in town. Or her if you was leaving."

Womack had never seen a man change as suddenly as Chapman did in the next instant. He seemed to grow smaller, to shrivel under Womack's stare. A moment before he had been strong-willed and dominant. Now he was trembling; a muscle in his cheek began to throb with the regularity of a pulse beat.

"Get this straight," Chapman said in a low voice. "Everything I do is for Nita, and I'll do anything to please her. Some men want power and money for what they'll do for him. I ain't that way. I just want to please Nita. Can you savvy that?"

Womack nodded. "She looks like she's worth pleasing."

"I worship her," Chapman went on. "It ain't just loving her. It's more'n that. I aim to build the CC into the biggest cattle empire in Colorado. I'll do anything and I'll use anybody to do the job." He threw out his hand in a pleading gesture. "Stay away from her, Womack. Just stay away."

"I ain't a wife stealer."

Chapman looked up at Womack as if measuring his sincerity. Then he rose, his mouth grim, as if regretting he had given Womack this glimpse of his soul. He said, "If you are, I'll kill you, and I don't give a damn whether you're the great Womack or not. I'm looking ahead, a long ways ahead, and I know where I'm going."

He walked to the door, and it was only then that Womack saw that his left leg was short and that the foot turned out. In those few moments Womack had learned a great deal about Cole Chapman. His wife was both his weakness and his strength. For her he could be tough and brutal; without her he would be an undersized cripple, his life lacking direction.

Chapman put his hand on the doorknob and looked back. "Don't tell nobody what I said about Nita. Savvy?"

"I ain't a gabber."

Chapman nodded as if he believed him. "Have you made any plans?"

"No. What I do depends on a lot of things."

"I ain't a patient man," Chapman said irritably. "I pay well for a good job, but I won't pay a damned nickel for half a job. Come on. We'll find Nita."

Womack followed Chapman into the saloon, wondering why he wanted to find Nita, and not liking it. The other three, Womack saw, were gone. Garrity rose from the poker table, asking, "Want a drink, Cole?"

"No," Chapman said, and hurried on toward the batwings, his body dipping with each step of his short leg.

They went out into the sunlight, Chapman swinging toward the hotel. They reached it and stepped into the lobby. Chapman asked, "Nita upstairs?"

The clerk nodded. "I ain't seen her come down." He recognized Womack and motioned to the war bag. "Your room's 14."

Womack caught the key the clerk tossed to him and picked up his bag. Chapman was halfway up the stairs by the time Womack caught up with him.

"I didn't know you'd taken a room here," Chapman said, annoyance in his voice. "Garrity could have put you up in the Starlight."

"This is all right," Womack said, wondering why Chapman did not want him to stay there.

Chapman reached the hall ahead of Womack. He motioned to a door. "That's your room. Toss your war sack in and come on."

Womack opened the door and dropped his bag inside. Chapman had gone on to a door at the end of the hall. He waited until Womack caught up, then opened the door and went in, calling, "Nita."

There were two rooms, the first furnished as a parlor, with two rocking chairs, a walnut love seat, a carved mahogany center table, and a big piano that was set between the windows of the street wall. The floor was covered by a dark red carpet, so soft underfoot that it completely muffled Chapman's footsteps as he crossed the room. All the furnishings spoke of money loudly, but the over-all effect was one of studied elegance.

A door leading into the second room was open, and Womack saw that it was a bedroom. Nita stepped through the door, frowning until she saw Womack, then she smiled in the quick way of a woman who can change her mood at will.

"I didn't know you were here, Mr. Womack," Nita said. "I'm glad you and Cole got together. I'm hungry."

Chapman pushed his hands into his pockets. He didn't say anything for a moment, but Womack could feel the rage that gripped the man. It surprised Womack, for there seemed to be no reason for it.

"He ain't eating with us," Chapman said. "I'm going out to the ranch. You coming?"

"No. You could stay for supper, Cole. You know I like to eat here, and we don't get to town very often."

Nita's hands were fisted at her sides, her red lips were pulled thin against her white teeth. She stood a full head taller than her husband, a willowy woman in whom the love of reckless living ran like a clear strong stream. Her dark eyes were bent on Chapman. Womack, watching closely, sensed that hers was the stronger will, that Chapman felt his weakness and was holding back his unreasonable rage only by an effort.

"All right," Chapman said after a moment's silence. "We'll eat in town. I brought Womack along to tell you he can't eat supper with us. That's right, ain't it, Womack?"

"Looks like it," Womack said. "Thanks for the invitation, Mrs. Chapman."

She stopped Womack with a gesture. "Cole is a jealous man. I don't know why, because I have never given him any reason to be. Sometimes I think he wants me to stay out there on the ranch and rot. I won't do it, Cole. I just won't do it. You hear?"

"I hear," Chapman said in a tight voice, "but that's got nothing to do with this. Womack is working for the combine, and I don't aim for you to get him sidetracked. Go ahead and get your supper, Womack. The Chinaman across the street is a good cook."

Womack walked out and went down the stairs. Chapman's actions, he knew, had not been due to any fear that he would be sidetracked. Because the man was crazy as far as his wife was concerned, he would be both dangerous and unpredictable.

As Womack ate his supper, his distaste for the situation grew. Whether Nita had given Chapman any reason to be jealous was nothing to him. Chapman would know that, but he had pulled Womack into an unpleasant scene for no better reason than the humiliation of his wife in front of a stranger. That, to Womack's way of thinking, made Chapman a small man in spirit as well as in stature, and did not agree with his assertion that he worshiped his wife; or if he did, it was a self-centered egotistical kind of worship at best.

It was dusk when Womack stepped back into the street. Lights had come to life in the saloons and the hotel, and as he walked through the lobby he saw that Nita and Chapman were eating in the dining room, Nita's face stormy and hurt. Womack went up the stairs, wishing he could see Rose or her brother, for he had a feeling that there was much left untold, and that this situation between the Chapmans had a close relationship with the trouble that threatened the mesa.

Womack lighted the lamp on the bureau. The barren room was little different from other hotel rooms in cow towns where he had stayed. The furniture seldom varied: a straight-backed chair, a pine bedstead, and a white bureau with its cracked basin and pitcher of water. There were the usual crude drawings on the wall, the torn strips of wallpaper, even the bullet holes in the ceiling where some drunken cowhand had left his marks.

Womack moved to the window and rolled a smoke. He fired it, considering what Rose had said about justice. He had promised to do some thinking on the subject. Well, it was going to take a good deal of thinking, and he was sure it was a matter which Cole Chapman had never given a moment's thought. Chapman and Red Manion were men he could despise, and he doubted that Grant Hovey was worth the trouble it would take to keep him out of trouble. Womack's sympathy was with Ira Slade, the man Chapman had described as a worker, a stubborn man who wouldn't "listen good."

In the past Womack had never let his sympathy get in the way of his job, but it was getting in the way now because Rose had insisted that he think about justice. That was where the boot pinched. There was no justice in greedy men wanting more, even if it meant keeping Grant Hovey out of trouble, and that was the thing he had been hired to do.

A knock brought Womack around. He waited a moment until he heard the knock again, then crossed to the door and opened it, right hand on his gun. It was Black Garrity, the superficial smile on his thin lips.

"You can take your hand off your iron," Garrity said. "That's the trouble with fellows like you. The first thing you think about is your damned cutter."

"Come in," Womack said, and stepped aside.

Garrity walked through the door and sat down on the bed. "Shut the door, friend. I've got talk to make."

Womack obeyed, wondering what had brought the gambler here. He dropped into the chair and rolled a fresh smoke, finding himself reminded again of Nita Chapman when he looked at Garrity. She was taller and younger, but there was a close resemblance in their features. Nita's were perfect, giving her a haunting beauty that was startling, but Garrity's face held a sort of feminine perfection strangely at variance with the impression of tough masculinity that he gave.

"I'll get to the point," Garrity said, "and I'll see what you do with it. I know as well as you do that Cole didn't send for you. You horned into the play, and I'm wondering why."

Womack said nothing. He had assumed that Chapman and Garrity were very close in their relationship, a natural guess in view of the fact that Garrity had called himself Chapman's watchdog. It came as no surprise, then, that Chapman had told Garrity how it was.

"Well?" Garrity murmured.

"You're talking," Womack said. "I ain't."

"Then it's about time you were talking." Garrity's smile was gone now. "What do you think of Cole?"

"It ain't my job to think about him. He pays and I work, and that's the way it is."

"Sure, sure," Garrity said impatiently. "But you're no fool, Womack. When you work for a man, you size him up."

"Thanks," Womack said.

"You're a close-mouthed son." Garrity took a cigar from his pocket and bit off the end. "Well, I'll tell you what you thought. Here's a little man who's crippled and can't see good without his glasses, but he's the big gun on this range who's got a dirty job he wants done, so you'll make him pay and pay good."

"Keep talking. You ain't said much yet."

"And you've found out he's got a damned purty wife he's about to lose and he's out of his head over her. You've found out that's why he's pushing. He don't need any more range. He's just got to keep proving to his wife that he's big."

"He didn't say anything about losing her."

"He don't know it," Garrity said. "Not how bad it is; but he's afraid. That's a hell of a thing, Womack.

Cole should never have to be afraid. You see, I'm on his side. That's what I came in here for. I don't want you to forget it."

"You think I'm not on his side?"

"I know you're not. I'm a good guesser, Womack. It's my business to guess right. Now I know the Hovey kids. They hate Cole and they hate Nita. Maybe they've got a right to, Grant being what he is; but that isn't the point. I'm saying I'm on Cole's side. If you double-cross him, I'll kill you, Womack. I don't give a damn about rules. I'll use a shotgun and I'll blow your head off."

So Garrity had guessed the truth! That did surprise Womack, but he masked his face against it. He said easily, "So you think I'll double-cross Chapman. Why?"

"Damn it, I'll spell it out in little words, so you'll know. I put several things together: Ed going out to Denver; Rose coming in on the stage with you; Cole telling me he didn't send for you and that you didn't promise him a thing. Hell, you didn't even put a figure on the job. Now can you deny that Ed and Rose Hovey hired you?"

"You wouldn't believe me if I did."

"No, I guess I wouldn't." Garrity put the cigar into his mouth. "Now listen to me. You can have a good thing here, as good as I've got if you're willing to play watchdog. Cole isn't much by himself, but he's made himself a hell of a big man with a little help. Now there's two good things about him. He's got an eye for making money and he's loyal to them that stick with him. The Hovey kids can't do anything for you. Cole can."

"You aiming to tell Chapman what you've guessed?"

Garrity chewed on his cigar a moment, black eyes probing Womack. He said: "I'll wait a while. I want to see how you play your hand." He rose. "Come on. Nita wants to see you."

"Chapman told me to stay away from Nita."

"He'll overlook this. He trusts me." Garrity jerked his head at the door. "You've got to come or she'll come here."

Garrity crossed the room to the door. Womack hesitated. He had seen enough of Nita Chapman for one day, but he didn't want her in his room. He followed Garrity into the hall.

"Go ahead," the gambler said. "Knock on her door. I'll wait outside. Just don't stay all night."

Womack stepped past Garrity and tapped on Nita's door. She was playing the piano. She called, "Come in." When he opened the door, she said, "Sit down, Mr. Womack," and kept on playing.

Womack dropped down on the love seat. Nita was softly playing a haunting Spanish tune that he had heard along the border but could not name. He looked at the graceful curve of her neck, at her slim straight back; he saw the glow of the lamplight on her black hair, and he watched her fingers move smoothly across the white keys. She suddenly struck one crashing chord and whirled to face him.

"What do you think of my husband, Mr. Womack?" she asked in a high strained voice.

It was queer, Womack thought, that she should ask the same question Black Garrity had. He said, "It ain't my job to think about him."

"But you have," she cried. "You couldn't help it. You saw this evening what he is, a little miserable bug of a man who pretends to give me everything while he gives me nothing. I'm a woman, Womack, and I'm not ashamed of it, but I might as well not be married. Cole Chapman is not a man."

Womack sat very still, his hands on his knees. He watched her, and he was stirred by her as any man would have been stirred. She was wearing a white silk dress that revealed the firm curves of her breasts and hips, a provocative dress that a woman would wear only on a special occasion.

"Don't be shocked, Womack," Nita said. "There are times when I've got to talk or I'll go crazy. Listen to me. I've been married three years. I have this." She made a sweeping gesture. "I have all the clothes I need. I have a big house on the ranch and a woman to do my work. I should be happy, shouldn't I?" She laughed scornfully. "Well, I'm not."

She rose and came to him, walking gracefully, hips swaying a little, and sat down on the love seat beside him. "You're making a mistake, working for Cole. He'll use you and throw you away when the time comes. He'll do the same with the other men who are in the combine. He needs them to cover his ambition, but the day will come when Dillon Mesa will be CC range unless somebody stops him. I don't know what will happen to Hovey and Manion and Lowrie, but something happened to Lowrie's father."

She gave him a smile, a tight curve of her lips. "That's the way Cole Chapman works. No amount of money that he has promised to pay you will justify the things he'll have you do. Believe me, Womack. You should have seen that this evening. He wants to keep me for himself. Just to look at. That's all." She leaned toward him so that he felt the pressure of her breast against his shoulder. "I had the feeling that you were one man who wouldn't be afraid of him."

"It ain't exactly a proposition of being afraid," Womack said.

"Then maybe it's another proposition." She drew back, laughing scornfully. "I've always wondered about men who called themselves gunmen. Do you have blood in your veins, or ice water?"

He rose. He said uneasily, "I wouldn't have come in if I'd—"

"I know." She got up and faced him, her smile provoking. "It's money, isn't it? Just money, and when you sell your gun you sell your soul. Cole's your boss and Cole's my husband, or so the law says, and that means there will never be anything between us.

Well, Mr. Womack, that's just fine. There never would have been anything anyhow."

"You're a lot of woman," he said, "but Chapman's got his loop on you. If I judge him right, he ain't likely to let it go."

"Not as long as he's alive." She laid a hand on his arm. "Womack, I thought I could change any man's mind, but I see I'm wrong. I wanted you to promise you wouldn't go after Ira Slade. That's the first thing Cole will have you do."

"What's Slade to you?" Womack asked brutally.

She dropped her hand, color coming into her cheeks. "You have no cause to ask that. I have some decency, you know."

That was something he had been wondering about, but he didn't say it. Shrugging, he asked, "Well, why the interest in Slade's health?"

"You won't believe it, but I'll tell you," she cried passionately. "You'll bathe this mesa in blood, and for no reason except to make Cole Chapman a bigger man than he is. He's power crazy, Womack. He's got the mining camps contracted to use combine beef. He's got Paddy Ryan, the banker, tied up so he won't give the little ranchers any more loans. He's stopped credit at the stores. You know why? So people will kowtow to him and let him forget he's just a crippled mouse who can't see without his glasses."

Womack stood motionless, staring at her taut face. He said: "Chapman told me he worshiped you. Said everything he done was for you."

"He's a liar," she said in that same passionate tone. "There never was a minute when he didn't think of himself first. Take a look at yourself, Bill Womack, and at the man you're working for. You should be proud. Go out and see the kind of graze that Slade and his neighbors have. Cole has kept them off the good grass. See the shacks they live in and look at their hide-and-bone beef. Go out and kill Ira Slade, and then be proud."

He couldn't tell, watching emotion flow across her face, whether she meant it or not. With a woman like Rose Hovey he would have known, but he could not be sure of Nita. He said, "I'll take that look tomorrow, but I ain't sure I'll smoke Ira Slade down."

"If you don't, you'll never earn a nickel of Cole's money. Why don't you get out of the country, Womack? Just get out and leave us alone."

"I'll take that look first," he said, and left the room.

Garrity was still waiting in the hall. He walked with Womack to his room, saying, "Right persuasive, Nita is, when she wants to be. Did she persuade you?"

"No." Womack reached his room and went in. Garrity followed, his cigar tilted upward from his mouth. Womack asked irritably, "What the hell do you want now?"

"Why, I like to talk to a good listener," Garrity said, "and sometimes I like to ask questions. What do you think of the rest of the combine?"

"Damn you—"

Garrity held up his hand, smiling in his meaningless way. "Don't get hot, boy. I'll tell you, since you don't want to tell me. You figure Grant Hovey is a pretty poor stick, and Red Manion totes his star because Cole got it for him and Red likes to play the big sheriff, but you ain't sure about Lowrie, are you?"

"No, I ain't," Womack admitted.

"Now I'll tell you something. Nobody else is, either. He sits up there on the head of Ute Creek, watching everybody like a damned long-nosed hawk. Never says much, Lowrie don't. Just watches. Now was I you, I'd do some watching myself." Garrity nodded. "Good night." He went out and closed the door.

Womack lay awake a long time after he had gone to bed, his mind turbulent with the thoughts that raced through it. He understood now why young Ed Hovey had said he didn't know how things were. It had been the same with Rose, who had said somebody had lighted a fuse that would blow them all up. Was it Chapman who had touched the match to the fuse, the "miserable bug of a man," determined to show everybody that he was more than Nita thought he was? Or was it someone else who was responsible for Chapman's drive for power?

If Womack could stay alive, time would give him the answer. Then his mind turned to Rose, who thought in terms of right and wrong, of God and the devil, of justice and injustice, and he knew he had to stay alive. Not for the dollars that his gun could earn, but for Rose Hovey.

Chapter 5: Little Men's Range

WOMACK WOKE EARLY, BUT NOT BECAUSE THERE WAS ANY need to. It was an old habit that went back to his boyhood years, when he had earned his living on a Missouri farm by working all day and half the night. He dressed and shaved, straining his eyes in the early-morning light, for the mirror hanging above the bureau returned a wavy, distorted image.

When he went downstairs he saw that the dining room was still closed, so he moved on across the lobby to the street. He paused there on the boardwalk for a time, seeing the little tawdry cow town partly blanketed by the shrinking night shadows. He heard someone cutting wood behind the Chinaman's restaurant, the sound of the ax blows clear and sharp in the high thin air; he heard a rooster crow. A man coughed in the Starlight, then the batwings were flung out and the swamper sloshed a bucket of dirty water into the street dust and went back.

It was not a pretty town. It was not even a good town, for Womack was remembering the air of sleepy indolence that lay upon it the day before, when he had stepped down from the stage. At that moment the combine had been meeting; the men who had the best grass were scheming how to get more. In a way Cole Chapman epitomized the town and the powers who controlled the mesa. He was small and he wanted to be big; he was weak and he wanted everyone to think he was strong.

Womack crossed the street to the Chinaman's and found the restaurant open. The Chinaman came along the counter, bowing and greeting Womack in a sing-song voice, as if it were a great honor to have him there. Womack gave his order, and the Chinaman shuffled back into the kitchen.

It may have been the mood that was on Womack this morning, a strangely thoughtful mood for him; or it may have been the deep weariness that a night of troubled sleep had not lifted. Whatever the cause, a depression lay upon him. Everything he saw reminded him of Cole Chapman or of Chapman's influence. Now it was the Chinaman who brought his meal, still bowing and scraping in a subservient manner that a free man should never use. Perhaps it was the Chinaman's way, or perhaps it was the slavish polite-ness that Chapman demanded for himself and those who worked for him.

Womack finished his meal and went outside. The sun was well up now, the San Juan peaks still misty with shadow, the La Sals far to the west bright with the morning. Womack rolled a smoke and fired it, but he found no pleasure in the cigarette. He threw it into the street and turned toward the livery stable. Then he saw the old man moving across the street to him, and he waited.

"You're Bill Womack, ain't you?" the man asked as he stepped up on the boardwalk.

"That's right."

"I'm Paddy Ryan." The old man held out a clawlike hand. "I own the bank and Cole Chapman owns me."

Womack shook Ryan's hand, surprised by his frankness. He said, "I've heard of you."

"I'll bet you have," Ryan said. "I'll bet they told you in the meeting yesterday about how the little fellows didn't have no more credit. Yes, sir, that tickles Cole. Makes him feel as big as all hell." He jerked his head at the Starlight. "Come on. Let's have a drink. I want to talk. I might even listen while you tell me how you got to be so damned big."

Womack grinned. "I couldn't tell you that. Ain't real sure myself."

They crossed the street to the Starlight, the old man saying: "I've met a lot of 'em in my day, Womack, and my day goes back a long ways. I seen Dodge City when it was roaring. Abilene. Ogallala. The Black Hills camps. Tombstone. I've seen most of the big boys. Hickock. Earp. Masterson. Thompson. Hardin. Yes, sir, the bad ones and the good ones, and only God and the devil know which was which."

Ryan pushed through the batwings. The swamper looked up from the back of the room, calling, "We ain't open yet."

"You've got liquor, ain't you, Bucky?" Ryan asked. "Go on with your sopping up."

Ryan moved behind the bar and brought a bottle and two glasses back to Womack. "You're a new one. Now they claim you're fast, but whether you're as fast as the old ones is something to auger about. No way to tell. Most of the boys I knew has cashed in their chips from lead poisoning. If you stick with the business, you'll be doing the same."

Ryan filled the glasses and put the bottle down. He was a very tall man with yellow crepe skin and a thin white beard that fluttered as he talked. Womack guessed that he was close to seventy, but he stood very straight, and his dark eyes were clear and sharp and probing.

"Here's mud in your eye," Ryan said, and lifted his glass.

They drank and put their glasses back on the mahogany, Ryan bringing the back of a bony hand across his mouth. He said: "I just wanted to swap a little talk with another slave. I've been a gambler most of my life. Well, sir, I came here with a little money and I started a bank. I didn't have enough when times got tight, so Cole bought in. That's why he plays the fiddle and I gotta dance to his tune." He gave Womack a straight look. "Funny thing. I'm respectable now, but you ain't. You know that, don't you?"

"It don't worry me," Womack said.

Ryan snorted. "The hell it don't. Take last night. I heard Mrs. Chapman invite you to supper, but Cole and his wife et without you and you et at the Chinaman's. You know why? You just ain't respectable. Maybe Nita never thought of it, but Cole did."

Womack waved it aside, not wanting the old banker to know how painful the wound was that he had probed. It was of no use to lie to Ryan again about his lack of respectability not worrying him. He said: "Thanks for the drink. I'll be riding—"

"Not yet you ain't," Ryan said. "I ain't got my talking done. I aim to tell you about Chapman. I never seen a little fellow like him get so far, but he didn't do it by himself. He's had help from me and Red Manion and this fellow Garrity. And his ramrod, Todd Jarvis. Now you come along. I'd say you were just a deuce, but you fill out his hand. Smart, Cole is. Never misses a bet."

"What the hell are you driving at?"

Ryan filled the glasses and put the bottle down. "Where you riding today?"

"I want to see Ira Slade."

"Cole wants him dead. Gonna do the job today?"

"No."

"Then what you riding out there for?"

"I want to see what kind of a hairpin he is."

Ryan picked up his glass and put it back again. He stared at the amber liquor for a time, right hand running absently back and forth across the smooth mahogany. Then he said in a low tone: "Funny how some men play their cards. I always dealt a fair hand, figuring that I could outguess the other fellow. If I couldn't, I didn't deserve to win; but Cole ain't that way. He don't bet unless he's got a sure thing. I trail along, hating him and hating myself and never finding the guts it takes to buck him." Ryan gave Womack a straight look. "Know why I'm telling you this?"

"No."

"I saw you yesterday when you got off the stage. You'd been riding in from Colatas with Rose Hovey. She and her brother Ed are about the only ones hereabouts who ain't afraid to say what they think of Cole and his way of doing things. So I made a bet with myself. If Rose knew who you were, she'd tell you what she thought. She just ain't afraid of nothing or nobody, Rose ain't. If she did tell you, well, that was the bet: whether you'd string along with Cole."

It was like watching a play, Womack thought, and he was the audience. He saw each actor come on the stage, one after another, and he had to draw his conclusions about them as he saw them. A single mistake might be a fatal one. He could be reasonably sure about Rose and her brother. And about Garrity, for the gambler had made his position clear. Ryan might have been sent by Garrity to get him to talk. Perhaps the gambler was in the back room now, a cocked gun in his hand. If Womack said the wrong thing, there was a good chance he would not walk out of here alive.

"Pay yourself off," Womack said irritably. "You lost the bet. I'll play along with Chapman for a while."

Ryan lifted his glass, his voice mocking: "To a brave man, Womack. If you're able to ride back to town after you see Ira, I'll buy you another drink."

Nodding curtly, Womack swung on his heel and strode out of the saloon. He had a feeling that treachery was all around him, and he wondered if Cole Chapman, depending on so many others, ever felt any real peace of mind.

Womack rented a livery-stable horse and took the west road out of town. A mile from Dogdance he swung south, following a long ridge that broke off sharply on the west side. It was better, he decided, to stay off the road. He had no illusions about that. It was doubtful if Slade would listen to him, and he was reasonably sure that Slade, striking back at the combine, had ordered the Pierson boys to watch the stage station and turn back anyone who looked like a gun fighter.

Now that Joe Pierson was dead, Lud would put the killing in the worst light he could. If Slade and his neighbors got the upper hand, they'd put a rope on Bill Womack's neck and have him swinging from a limb in a matter of minutes; but it was a risk he had to take. There was always the danger, in an explosive situation like this, that Slade and his bunch would be forced by Chapman's pressure to make a move. Once the guns began sounding, there would be no stopping them short of final defeat of one side or the other; and the law, such as it was on Dillon Mesa, would back the combine.

Before Womack had gone three miles, he saw what Nita had meant by telling him to go out and see the kind of graze that Slade and his neighbors had. He could look back over the range that the combine claimed, a tawny carpet of rich grass that swept eastward to the foothills. To the west was a broken country of canyons and small mesas that he had seen from the road the day before. To say that this was poor graze was an understatement. There was runty sage-

brush and some dwarf cedars, but very little grass of
any kind. It was hardscrabble range, the leavings that
the late comers like Ira Slade had been forced to take.
It had been poor originally and it was worse now, for
it was overgrazed to the place where it would produce
exactly what Nita had said, hide-and-bone cattle.

By midmorning Womack was seeing a few skinny
steers. Even the brands were sloppy, burned on by
hand-shaped irons. He saw the Lazy S, Slade's brand,
and some others he didn't know. He rode down off the
ridge he had been following into a brush-choked
canyon, its bed dry, and climbed out. It was then that
he saw the first shack, a slab shed with a pole corral
behind it. There was no sign of life about the place.

Womack had secured directions from the stableman
before he had left Dogdance, so he was sure that this
was not Slade's ranch. He went on, still angling
southwest. Hell's Wall rose directly south of him now,
a sheer red cliff, as Rose had described it, effectively
blocking off the little ranchers from the high-country
summer range. There was nothing here worth fighting
for, and Womack could not dislodge the thought from
his mind that Chapman was too smart a man to fight
for something that would be useless after he had it. It
was possible that Chapman didn't want this grass,
that he was determined to wage a preventive war to
keep Slade's bunch from reaching out for the good
graze to the east. There was the other possible explanation, too, the crazy quirk in Chapman's make-up
that forced him to insist on having everything whether
it was worth having or not. If that was the answer,
there was no telling where Chapman would stop, for a
man like that reached and kept reaching until he was
dead or beaten.

It was nearly noon when Womack rode up out of
another canyon to a bench where the grass was better
than it had been for miles. There was a neat log cabin
fifty yards in front of him, with a garden, a couple of
young cottonwoods in front, and a small barn and

several corrals on beyond the house. From the description the stableman had given him, Womack was certain that this was Slade's Lazy S.

Womack rode directly toward the cabin, knowing that the next few minutes would decide his success or possibly his death. It was a familiar situation to him, risky, but something he could not avoid if he did the job he had set out to do. There was some value in taking the bold way, for it usually disarmed suspicion.

Dismounting at the log trough, Womack watered his horse, then took a drink from the pipe that fed the trough from a spring on the hillside to the north. He finished, and lifting his head, saw that a man had come out of the cabin and was watching him intently.

Womack looped the reins over the hitch pole and moved toward the cabin, asking, "Are you Slade?"

The man nodded, his gaze dropping to the gun on Womack's hip and coming back to his face. "I'm Slade. Looking for a bait of grub?"

Slade had mistaken him for a grub-line rider, a common mistake and one that suited Womack. He said: "I'm hungry and I can pay. I ain't looking for a handout."

He was close to the rancher now, and he made his mental judgment of the man. Slade was tall and whittled down by countless hours of riding until he was all bone and hard muscle. He was wearing a clean shirt and pants, and his hair was combed. Probably ready to eat, Womack thought. He stopped ten feet from Slade, and stood there, his eyes meeting the man's probing gray ones.

"I'm wondering if you're Womack," Slade said at last.

"That's right."

"Chapman sent you to kill me, didn't he? You'll tell me to get a gun and you'll give me an even draw just to ease your conscience, then you'll drill me like you done Joe Pierson."

Womack shook his head. "No. I came here to talk.

You've got the wrong slant about my ruckus with the Piersons. If I hadn't plugged Joe, him and Lud would have got me."

"That ain't the way Lud tells it," Slade said. "You ain't welcome here, Womack. We're burying Joe this afternoon."

Womack was silent for a moment, searching for words that might break down the man's fear and suspicion of him, but the words would not come. He knew how it was with Slade, and he could not blame him.

"I'm hungry," Womack said finally. "I'm not here to make trouble. I'm here to stop it."

Slade laughed harshly. "I'm likely to believe that. You're off your reservation, Womack. Go back and get Chapman and Hovey and the rest of 'em. Burn us out and kill our women and steal our cattle. That'll do the job, Womack."

Womack cuffed back his Stetson, wondering if he should tell the truth. He asked tentatively, "You know Rose and Ed Hovey?"

"Yeah, I know 'em and I know Grant. They don't come no lower'n Grant, Womack."

"Not Rose and Ed."

"Mebbe so. Mebbe not. We don't trust nobody, Womack. We can't. We've borrowed money from Paddy Ryan for years, and we've always paid up. Now he says we're bad risks. We've run bills at the stores in Dogdance, and we've always paid up. Now they say no more credit." Slade jabbed an accusing finger at Womack. "Finally he sends you."

"Fetch him in," a woman called from inside the cabin. "If he's hungry we'll feed him, and he can go on. No sense standing out there augering."

Slade shrugged. "That's my wife for you. Soft-hearted! Hell, I'd let you starve. Come on."

Slade turned and went inside. Womack followed, taking off his hat. A big woman standing at the stove turned and gave Womack a searching look. She said:

"So you're the great Womack. You don't look no different than fifty men who have ridden by here on their way to Utah, trying to beat the Colorado law."

"Law." Slade snorted his derision. "Red Manion's law, you mean?"

Mrs. Slade turned back to the stove. "No. I meant honest law."

Womack saw that they had eaten. Dirty dishes were on the table; the smell of cooked food lingered in the room. As far as Womack could see, the woman was making no effort to fix a meal for him. He stood beside the table uncertainly, his hat held at his side. Slade was on the other side of the table from him, hands in his pocket. He said in a cranky voice: "Hustle with his grub, Lois. I'll go hitch up. We've got to roll if we're gonna get to the burying."

Slade took a step toward the door. Womack turned toward him. "I can go without grub till I get back to Dogdance. I rode out here to ask you not to start the ball. I've got a hunch things will change."

Slade turned back, grinning derisively, and at that moment Womack's back was to the woman. Something in Slade's lean face warned him, and he started to whirl. He glimpsed the shadow of the descending frying pan and started to duck, then it caught him squarely on the head and sent him to the floor in a crashing fall.

Womack did not entirely lose consciousness. He fell on his face, and Slade was on him at once, pulling his hands behind him and tying them with a piggin' string. The woman was yelling: "Get off him, Ira. I'll kill him for his soft lying talk."

Her voice beat against Womack's ears through the rolling throbs of pain. Then Slade was tying his ankles and he was saying: "No. We'll let him lie there, and I'll fetch the boys back. We'll take him to town come dark and we'll hang him. I want Chapman to see his carcass."

"You're a fool," the woman stormed. "We haven't got any place to lock him up. He'll get away, and then where'll you be?"

"I know how to tie a man," Slade snapped. "Now, take a look. He'll be here till hell freezes over."

Outside a man called, "Ira. You here?"

Slade walked to the door. "Yeah, I'm here, but I'm ready to pull out. Just got me a bear by the tail and I turned him inside out."

"And he's leaving the critter alive," Mrs. Slade called. "He'll regret it ten times over before this is done."

"Who'd you get?" the man asked.

"Womack," Slade answered.

"The hell! Cole won't like that."

"Didn't figure he would," Slade said complacently. "I'll put his horse in the barn and hitch up. We've got to git."

"Wait a minute, Ira. This puts a different light on things. I don't know what you're figuring on, but if you give Manion an excuse to move in, you're in a tight. That's what Cole's been waiting for."

"Let 'em come," Slade shouted. "Let 'em come. We can't stand no more."

"You're making a mistake," the man said. "If you're gonna buck the law, why don't you go after Cole?"

"This is better," Slade said. "The Lord delivered Womack into our hands. Chapman will change his mind when he sees his tough hand hanging from a cottonwood limb."

Slade and his wife left the cabin, Mrs. Slade still saying that it was crazy to leave Womack there. Slowly and painfully Womack lifted his head. Red light danced before his eyes, but through it he was able to make out the man who was sitting his saddle in front of the cabin. It was big hawk-nosed Abner Lowrie.

Chapter 6: At Slade's

OVER WHAT SEEMED A GREAT DISTANCE, THE RATTLE OF A buggy leaving the yard came to Womack's ears; he heard the drum of hoofs as Lowrie rode away. The red light kept dancing before his eyes like the steady explosion of fireworks, and his head ached with throbbing beats of pain that were as regular as the rhythm of a pulse.

He heard Slade's words over and over, like a chanted refrain, "We'll take him to town come dark and we'll hang him." He had to get away! Had to! Had to! They'd hang him if he didn't. Chapman wasn't worth dying for. Neither was Grant Hovey. Just get away. Get away. He rolled over, and then he must have fainted, for afterward there was a period of time which he could not account for.

The next thing Womack felt was the stabbing sunlight in his eyes. It was late afternoon now, and the sun had moved westward so that the light fell through a window directly upon him. He rolled away from it and kept turning until he reached the wall. The red light was gone; his head was clearer now, with only a steady dull pain instead of the throbbing hammer strokes.

It came back to him at once: Mrs. Slade hitting him with the frying pan, Ira Slade promising to hang him, and Abner Lowrie outside on his horse urging Slade to go after Cole Chapman—Lowrie, who had not said a word at the combine meeting. It was wrong, all wrong, Lowrie being here. Womack could not make an intelligent guess why the man had come, but one thing was certain: he was selling the combine out. That fact

could not be questioned, and it made Lowrie the kind
of man Womack hated above all others.

Womack managed to raise himself so that his back
was to the wall. He put his head against a log, his
immediate danger sweeping everything else from his
mind. He heard the steady, metallic beat of a clock
somewhere in the room. It took him a minute to
locate it; then he saw it on a shelf and strained his eyes
to make out the time. Four o'clock! Fear struck at him.
It ran down his spine and spread out through his belly
and for that moment panic made him helpless. He sat
there frozen, feeling the futility of any effort he might
make, knowing that Ira Slade would do exactly what
he said if he found him here after he returned from the
burying.

Womack could not guess when Slade would return
with his neighbors. He did not know the distance to
the Pierson place or the hour when the funeral was to
be held. He did know that the bulk of the afternoon
was gone and that he had been tied by an expert.
There was no give in the string that held his wrists and
his ankles, and to struggle against it would accomplish
nothing except to wear the skin off his wrists and
stiffen them.

Reason slowly crept back into his mind, and some
of the panic left him. He might have been there several
minutes, possibly an hour. Carefully he searched the
cabin for a knife, an ax, or even a piece of broken
glass. Any sharp edge would do if he could get his back
to it, but apparently there was nothing.

It was not a large cabin. There was a bed at one end
and a bureau that showed the scars of much moving;
there was the table with its dirty dishes, a stove, a
couple of homemade chairs, a bench, and a double-
barreled shotgun laid across a set of deer antlers on
the wall. There were cans and sacks of food on shelves;
the frying pan that Mrs. Slade had used to knock him
down was on the stove, together with a few other pots;

but there was nothing that would do the job. Womack
knew that the Slades must have a butcher knife, but he
could not see one. He thought of the ax again. It would
be outside, probably sticking into the chopping block.
If it was double-bitted, there would be a sharp edge
held firmly upright that would free Womack if he
could get his back to it.

He worked his way to the door, rolling over and
over, then angled around so that his head was on the
threshold. He crawled out like a measuring worm,
lifting the front of his body and falling forward. It
seemed like an eternity before he was through the
door. He lay motionless for a time, panting, sweat
bursting through his skin, the afternoon sun full upon
him. It seemed fantastically hot for so late in the year.

He began to roll again, across the front of the cabin
and around the end until he reached the chip pile.
When he saw the ax, a sense of final failure washed
through him. It had been tossed on top of the wood-
pile, whether by accident or foresight on Slade's part
he didn't know. Either way, it was out of his reach.
Suddenly he heard a horse crossing the flat. He
supposed it would be Slade, coming back alone to get
him. Here he was, as helpless as a trapped animal.
Then he remembered that Slade had left in a buggy.
Lowrie maybe! But that would be no help, not if
Lowrie was selling the combine out.

Womack rolled closer to the wall of the cabin and
pressed against it. He wondered if this was the end of
his twine. Again that queasy fear worked down into
his belly, and sweat formed a clammy film on his face.
What a hell of a way to die!

The horse reached the front of the cabin and
stopped. A man called, "Anybody here?"

It was a vaguely familiar voice. Not Lowrie's. Then
Womack remembered. It was the old banker, Paddy
Ryan. Womack yelled, "Here. Back here," and he was
weak with the sense of relief that ran through him.

It seemed an hour before Ryan reached the corner,

although it could not have been more than a matter of seconds. He looked down at Womack, a grin breaking across his craggy face. "Well, now, if you don't look like a calf waiting for a hot iron."

"Cut me loose, damn it," Womack yelled. "What are you standing there for?"

Still grinning, Ryan fished a knife out of his pocket and slashed the string. Womack got up, reeling a little until he put his back to the cabin wall. He stretched, flexing the muscles of his arms and rubbing his wrists. He asked, "How come you showed up out here?"

"Well, sir," Ryan said. "I've had myself quite a time. I knowed you had no business riding out here alone and I was purty sure you'd run into trouble, knowing Ira Slade like I do, so finally I got brave and made up my mind to have a look-see."

"Come on." Womack squinted up at the sun. "They'll be back before long, and we've got to be ready."

"I don't aim to wait for 'em," Ryan said quickly. "I ain't real popular hereabouts."

"You'll wait," Womack said. "I've got a few things to tell Slade and that woman of his."

Womack strode around the cabin to Ryan's horse, not waiting for the banker, and led the animal into the barn. He tied him in a stall next to the one that held the livery-stable mount he had ridden, loosened the cinch, and then returned to the cabin, where Ryan was standing in the irresolute manner of a bird about to take flight.

"Now you look here," Ryan began. "I saved your hide, but that's no reason for you to get me into a jackpot—"

"I'm beholden to you," Womack cut in. "I was a goner if you hadn't shown up, but we ain't running. We've got work to do. Let's get inside."

Ryan followed him into the cabin, moving slowly and reluctantly, and inclined to argue the matter. Womack said impatiently: "I made the mistake of giving my back to Mrs. Slade. Now quit worrying. I've done enough of it for both of us. Got a gun?"

"No."

Womack took the shotgun off the wall, saw that it was loaded, and handed it to the banker. "We'll wait for 'em. Takes the salt right out of a man when he looks into the muzzle of a scattergun."

"I ain't a real brave man," Ryan said resignedly as he took the shotgun, "and I kind o' like Ira Slade."

"I don't," Womack said. "I don't like his woman, neither."

"How'd you get into that fix?"

Womack told him, adding bitterly: "That's what comes of trying to help a damned fool who don't want to be helped. It wouldn't have happened if I'd smoked him down."

Ryan pulled at his beard, eyes thoughtful. "It wouldn't help your reputation none if I told around how I found you. Always seemed to me a gunman's reputation is the biggest asset he's got."

"Then don't tell it."

"I'm wondering," Ryan said softly. "I was wondering last night when Garrity came over to see me. He's an honest man, that Garrity. You always know where he stands. He'll go along with Cole because it pays him. I kind o' admire that kind of honesty."

Womack stood at the front window, his back to Ryan. He said: "Maybe you don't admire a man who ain't what he seems to be. That it?"

"That's it. There's even times when I don't admire myself. Cole needs whittling down. That's why I rode out here. Figured maybe you aimed to do a little whittling."

"What about this Abner Lowrie?"

"Well, now, I can tell you one thing. He ain't honest like Garrity. His dad was a regular old heller. Looked for a while like he might be the big gun on this range till one day he got himself dry-gulched. After that, Cole spread out and Abner, he just hangs on up there near the head of Ute Creek. Got some water rights, raises a little alfalfa, and runs a few head of cattle."

"What does he think?"

Ryan laughed softly. "That's a question, boy. No-body knows what goes on behind that big beak of his. Don't talk much, Abner don't. Just grins and looks at you, but mostly he listens."

"He was out here a while ago," Womack said, and told the banker about it.

Ryan was silent for a time, then he said, "I wonder."

Womack swung away from the window. "You wonder what?"

"It don't rightly make sense," Ryan went on, as if he hadn't heard Womack's question. "When a fellow is in the cattle business and his pa was in the cattle business before him, why, it don't make sense that he'd want to fetch in a swarm of clodbusters."

"You're the one who don't make sense," Womack said irritably. "Tell the rest of it."

"I know, I know. It's crazy, but I remembered it because it surprised me, coming from a fellow like Abner, who never said much. It was before old Jake died and before Cole got too big for his britches. Abner had been away to school. Old man Lowrie had some powerful ideas for his boy. It was the day he got back, and him and me was riding out to the Slash Triangle. His dad had sent word he wanted to see me, and in them days you jumped when old Jake Lowrie hollered just like you jump now when Cole hollers."

"How come Abner don't count for so much around here now?"

Ryan shrugged. "There's several tales about that. One allows it was a poker game that Abner got into with Cole after old Jake was shot, and Cole wound up with most of the Slash Triangle cattle. Another says Abner don't like to work, so he sold off most of his stock to Cole. I dunno. But what I was going to tell you was, there me and Abner was riding along, Abner looking back over the mesa. Real pretty up there close to the mountains. Seems like the land goes on and on, good land you could use to raise anything, and Abner says, 'Paddy, a man would be a millionaire if he could put water on the mesa and get it settled.'

"Well, sir, you could have blowed me out of the saddle with one good whiff. Old Jake would have died, hearing that, or Cole, or any of 'em. I says, 'Where'd you get a notion like that?' Then he clammed up, got red in the face, and didn't say a damned word all the rest of the way to the Slash Triangle."

Womack turned to the window again. He said, "What's that got to do with Lowrie being out here?"

"Maybe nothing. I told you it didn't make sense, but suppose Abner never forgot that idea. Long as Cole runs things hereabouts, he can't do nothing; but if he could bust Cole, maybe get him into a range war and get him killed so nobody would wonder about it, he could go ahead. I told you he had the water rights; and he's got the best spot for a dam there is on the mesa, just a little piece below his house."

There was no time to think about it then. They came up out of the canyon to the east, six riders, Slade and Lud Pierson in front. Womack said in a low voice: "They're coming. Don't let 'em know we're here. We'll throw down on 'em when they walk in."

Womack drew his gun and cocked it. Ryan stood beside him, facing the door, the hammers of his shotgun back. There was some talk as the riders reined up in front and dismounted, Lud Pierson's voice coming clearly to Womack: "I wish you'd have fetched him along, Ira. Would have been something to see, having him dance his way to hell right there over Joe's grave."

"Ain't too late, Lud," Slade said. "He's right here—" They trooped in, Slade leading. He stopped, staring at the place where he had left Womack. "He's gone."

"That's right," Womack said. "Hoist 'em, boys."

They wheeled to face Womack and Ryan, blinking in the gloom of the cabin. Their hands came up slowly, Pierson cursing in a low, bitter voice.

"That's fine," Womack said. "I don't want to drill any of you but Pierson, and I don't give a damn about him."

"Me, neither," Ryan said. "Buckshot sure messes a carcass up, don't it, Lud?"

"Damn you, Womack," Slade cried. "Lois was right. I should have let her beat your head off."

"And I should have smoked you down and stayed away from your woman." Womack motioned with his left hand. "Drop your gun belts, then step back."

They obeyed sullenly, Slade putting his eyes on Ryan. "So you ain't satisfied to use your bank. You've got to ride out here and point my own shotgun at me. Why don't you go back and crawl under a rock, Ryan?"

"Well, sir, this ain't my idea," the banker said. "I rode out here to see how Womack was making out and I found him tied up. He talked me into staying."

The six of them were lined up against the wall, their hands over their heads, and all showed the fear that was gripping them. Womack kicked their gun belts into the corner and stepped back to stand beside Ryan. He said, "You were fixing to hang me on Pierson's say-so, weren't you, Slade?"

The Lazy S owner licked dry lips and glanced sideways at Pierson. He said: "Yeah, that's what I aimed to do, but you can bet on one thing: if I get out of this, I won't make the mistake of leaving you alive again."

"Maybe you won't get out of this. If you was in my place, you'd smoke me down, wouldn't you?"

"That's sure as hell what I'd do," Slade blurted. "What do you expect, a gun slinger with your reputation coming in—"

"All right," Womack said testily. "Pierson didn't give you the straight of it." Womack told him how it had been, adding, "If you hadn't been so boogery you couldn't think straight, you'd know I wasn't after you, or I'd have burned you down when I first rode up."

"He's lying," Pierson cried. "He's lying right from the word 'go.'"

Womack lined his gun on the big man. "Pierson, there's one question you're going to answer. Who sent you to Moran's?"

"I ain't answering no questions," Pierson said sullenly.

"I think you will," Womack said. "I'll give you ten seconds to make up your mind. If you don't start talking, I'll start shooting."

There was little about Womack's grim face now that would have made anyone think he was an ordinary range drifter. Pierson must have seen the change; he didn't wait for the ten seconds. He screamed: "Don't plug me like this, Womack. You ain't that kind of a killer. Not if the things they say about you are true."

"Then answer my question."

Pierson's Adam's apple bobbed up and down for a moment, then he said in a low voice, "Abner Lowrie paid me to watch Moran's and turn back any gun slingers who were coming in to work for Chapman."

Rose had guessed it was Ira Slade who had stationed the Piersons at Moran's, and Womack had assumed she was right. But now he believed Pierson, for it would take money to hire men like the Piersons; and Slade and his neighbors plainly had no money.

Womack nodded at Slade. "Your turn. What was Lowrie doing out here, trying to talk you into going after Chapman?"

"He don't like Chapman's way of doing things, but he always gets outvoted at the combine meetings. He's the only friend we've got on the other end of the mesa." Slade glared at Ryan. "Even them that we thought was friends turned out to be double-crossing sons of—"

"Are we now," Ryan murmured. "Ever think you might be wrong, Ira?"

"Wrong, hell," Slade shouted with the deep bitterness of an injured man. "We've kept our noses clean, but Chapman accuses us of stealing combine beef. Lies, Ryan, and you know it. There ain't nothing out here the combine needs or wants. Well, we ain't standing for no more of it. We're going after Chapman like Lowrie says, and you can tell Chapman that."

"Did it ever occur to you that Lowrie is playing his own game?" Womack asked.

"He's on the level. Don't try to tell me anything else." Slade started to lower his hands. "I'm getting tired. How about—"

"Keep 'em up," Womack ordered. "I'll make you a deal. Slade, is your word good?"

"I'll make no deal with a hired gunhand," Slade shouted. "To hell with you."

"You ain't in much of a position to auger. I rode out here for two reasons. One was to see what sort of a hairpin you were. Now I've seen, and I don't like you, Slade. You're a stubborn, chuckleheaded fool, but that ain't the point. A man's got a right to his home, and that puts Chapman in the wrong."

"Who the hell are you working for?" Slade demanded. "A man like you don't go around trying to find out who's in the wrong."

Womack gave him a thin smile. In the past Slade would have been right, but the past was gone; he had cut it off just as he had known he would. Now he felt an inner satisfaction in what he was doing, and he hoped that Rose Hovey would some day know that.

"I'm sitting in the judgment seat," Womack said, "deciding on what folks call justice. Ever hear of it, Slade?"

"Sure I have, but if there is any justice—"

"I said I had a proposition, and I asked you if your word was good."

Slade looked along the line of men beside him, hesitating, then brought his gaze to Womack again. "It's good if I give it."

"That's better. The other reason I rode out here was to get you not to start the ball, and I figured you might take it into your head to do something like that. There's something wrong on this range, and I aim to find out what it is."

"To hell with you," Slade bellowed. "Hold off and let Chapman fetch his crew in and burn us out? Not much. We'll hit him first while we're together. If we wait, he'll get us one at a time."

Womack shook his head. "He's been waiting. Ain't no reason for him not waiting a little longer. Give me forty-eight hours, Slade."

"Better do it," Ryan said. "If this goes like I think it will, I'll see you boys through the winter. Cutting you off wasn't my idea."

"What makes you think I'll take your word on anything?" Slade demanded, his eyes pinned on Womack's face.

"You'll have to," Womack said flatly. "It's that or nothing as far as you're concerned."

A man at the end of the line said: "He's right, Ira. Won't hurt to wait that long."

Slade took a long ragged breath. "All right, Womack. You've got my word."

"Outside." Womack jerked his head at the door. "We're taking a walk. Ryan, get our horses."

They moved into the yard, Pierson grumbling that Slade was as crazy as a man could get. Womack let him talk, waiting in front of the cabin, the dying sun to his back. Ryan brought the horses, and Womack mounted, saying: "Leave the scattergun here. Slade, turn your horses loose. I ain't of a mind to be chased."

Slade sullenly obeyed. Womack fired a shot over the

horses, yelling at them and heading them west toward
a brushy draw that broke off a quarter of a mile
beyond the cabin. Ryan had mounted, and Womack,
with Ryan beside him, herded Slade and the others
across the flat and down into the canyon to the east.

"It'll take us all night to get them horses," a man
said complainingly.

"I didn't make no deal," Pierson shouted. "I'll get
you, Womack. I don't care how big a reputation
you've got. I'm gonna get square for Joe if it takes me
the rest of my life."

"I won't be hard to find." Womack glanced at his
watch. "It's six o'clock, Slade. You can figure forty-
eight hours from now. Don't forget one thing. Red
Manion may not be able to prove you're stealing
combine beef, but if you start throwing lead at Chapman he won't need to bother about proving anything."

Slade stood in the shadow of a runty cedar, back
straight, his bitter eyes on Womack. "I just know one
thing, Womack. I don't hire a gunhand to do my
fighting for me. A man can stand so much, and I've
stood it."

"There's different kinds of gunhands," Womack
said, "and I ain't Lud Pierson's stripe. If you work
him over, you might find out something about Lowrie
that'll surprise you."

"I know who my friends are," Slade said somberly.
"We'll give you forty-eight hours, and the Lord help
you if you fetch a bunch in here before that time's
gone."

Womack reined his horse around and put him up
the east side of the canyon, Ryan beside him. When
they reached the top, he looked back. Slade and the
others were climbing laboriously out of the canyon.
Womack rode on, his mind turning to Rose Hovey
and her father, and the sense of satisfaction that had
been in him gave way to a new worry. The real job had

not been started, and forty-eight hours might not be long enough, but Ira Slade had been harried to the point where he was almost crazy. He would not have promised to wait any longer.

Chapter 7: Gunfire in the Night

THEY STRUCK DIRECTLY NORTHWARD, FOLLOWING A LONG ridge that reached like a finger toward Devil River, and at dusk they came to the stage road that ran between Dogdance and the Utah line. Westward the sun had dropped behind the La Sals, the last scarlet reminder of the day fading rapidly before the insweeping night.

Suddenly, and without any apparent reason for his remark, Paddy Ryan said: "You know, Womack, I like the Hovey kids. Ed ain't the kind you can lead around by the nose. And Rose, well, now, there's a woman who could make a man a fine wife. She's smart and pretty, and she'd give a man something to settle down for."

Womack glanced at Ryan, his face a pale blob in the twilight. He said: "Go ahead. Say the rest of it."

"Well, I was fishing for the answer to the question Slade asked back there. Just who are you working for?"

"What's that got to do with the Hoveys?"

"Might have quite a bit. If you was running true to style, you'd have plugged Slade and hit back for town instead of getting yourself into a jam like you done. Don't look like you're working for Chapman, and that's a fact."

"Suppose I ain't?"

"Then who is it? This gab about sitting in the judgment seat ain't your style."

"You don't know nothing about my style," Womack said irritably. "There's one thing I do regardless. When I'm paid to do a job, I deliver the goods."

"I can believe that." Ryan sighed. "Well, sir, now the Hovey kids have some good ideas. Like fetching in white-faced bulls and improving the range stock we've got hereabouts. There could be fifteen ranches where there's four now, and they could all make a good living with less cattle if it was worked right."

"You're taking a long time to say anything," Womack said.

"All right. I'll say it. I told you Garrity came to see me late last night. He'd been drinking some and he was worried. Seems like he made a guess that Rose and Ed are the ones you're working for. Now Grant ain't worth a damn. The kids know that, but they're bound to stick with him. After watching you perform back there at Slade's place, I figure Garrity's right. If he is, it puts a different light on the whole shebang."

Womack held his reply for a time. He sensed that Paddy Ryan was not so much Cole Chapman's slave as he appeared to be, and that his sympathies were plainly with Slade and his neighbors, just as any fair-minded man's would be; but there were too many threads in this trouble that Womack had not tied together. He was in no position to trust anyone except Rose Hovey.

"You'll have to make your own guess," Womack said at last. "In case I forgot to mention it, thanks for getting me out of a tight."

"Sure, sure. Well, I didn't expect an answer. A fellow like you learns to be close-mouthed, and I reckon it's for the best."

There was no more talk for a time. Darkness was complete except for the jagged streaks of lightning above the San Juans to the east. Clouds had moved across the sky, and the smell of rain was heavy in the air. Presently the lights of Dogdance showed ahead of them. Within half an hour they reached the town, and Womack reined up in front of the livery stable.

"I keep my horse at home," Ryan said. "See you in the morning?"

"I've got some riding to do."

"Well, don't let no more women crack you on the noggin with a frying pan," Ryan said, and rode on down the street.

The town was deathly quiet. It might mean nothing, for it was the middle of the week. If Dogdance was like most small cow towns, Saturday night would be the only time when it came to life. Perhaps the quiet was natural; but the years had developed a sort of sixth sense in Womack about such things, and an uneasiness now gripped him that seemed to have no real foundation in fact.

Womack left his horse in the stable and paid the hostler. When he left, he moved rapidly away from the cone of light that fell from the archway, eyes probing the street. One of the first things that his business had taught him was the simple fact that a little caution at the right time was a bigger help in staying alive than all the shells in his gun belt.

There were lights in the hotel, the three saloons, and the Chinaman's restaurant. Together with the lantern in the archway of the stable, they threw orange patches into the red dust of the street. Still there was no tangible evidence that danger was there, no sound, no movement; yet the warning remained in him.

This sensing of danger when there was nothing to see or hear was something he had never understood, but it had saved his life more than once. To anyone else it would have been a superstition to be disregarded; to Bill Womack it was a very real thing that could not be discounted.

There were a number of weed-covered lots across the street, spots of blackness between the lights.

Anyone watching from the cover of that blackness
would have seen him ride into town, would have seen
Ryan go on, and would have known that Womack
would go to his hotel. The moment he stepped into the
hotel lobby, he would be silhouetted against the light,
making a target that a man could not miss if he was
any good at all with a gun.

Womack waited, the minutes plodding by, his
nerves tightening with the passage of each minute.
Presently he realized that the warning which had
come to him had stemmed from the knowledge that
Garrity had been worried enough to go to Ryan with
his guess that Womack was working for Ed and Rose
Hovey. If he had done that, it was likely that he had
gone to Chapman with the same guess; and Chapman
was not a man to overlook deception. It was possible
that Garrity, having had a night and a day to think
about it, had decided to remove Womack himself.
And there was Nita, who defied analysis.

Womack might have waited five minutes or thirty.
He didn't know, for at a time like this each minute
became an hour. He was not a patient man. If
someone was waiting for him, the man was probably
better at waiting than he was. Womack pulled his gun
and moved on, hugging the dark front of a store. He'd
make the dry-gulcher show if there was one; but if his
imagination was building something out of nothing, it
was time he found out.

The hotel was directly ahead, lamplight from the
lobby falling across the walk and into the street from
two windows and the open door. Womack lunged in
front of the first window, bending low, and reached
the second. Then the shot came from directly across
the street, the slug taking a button off the front of
Womack's shirt and slashing through the hotel window.

Dropping flat, Womack squeezed off three shots,
spacing them two feet apart so that they covered the
place where the bushwhacker had stood. He held his

fire and waited, but there was no more shooting. The killer might have thought he had hit Womack, judging from the way he had gone down; or else, failing in his first shot, he had no stomach for a finish fight. Probably he'd tucked his tail and run.

It must have been a full minute before anyone showed on the street, then they came piling out of the saloons; but Womack didn't wait. He holstered his gun and ran into the lobby, ignoring the scared clerk's question, and went up the stairs on the run.

There was a line of light under Nita's door. He pounded on it, then waited while he heard a woman's heels tap across the floor. When the door swung open, Nita stood there, looking questioningly at him. He stared past her to where Garrity sat beside a window, realizing that the person who had shot at him could not have been either Nita or Garrity. There had not been enough time for either of them to run to the end of the block, cross the street, and come into the hotel from the back.

"Why, this is a surprise," Nita said. "Come in."

"Ain't got time," Womack said. "I was just wondering about something."

Womack started to turn, but stopped when Garrity called, "Wait," and came to the door. "What was the shooting about?"

"Somebody took a shot at me. He made the mistake of missing."

"So I see," Garrity murmured. "You thought it was Nita."

"Or you."

"Why, Mr. Womack," Nita said with deliberate malice, "I never use a gun on a man. I don't need to."

"But if your other weapons didn't work, you might use a gun."

Garrity gave him a lip-deep smile. "You're smart and you're hard to kill. I'm thinking it's too bad your dry-gulcher didn't shoot straight."

"I thought you'd figure that way," Womack said.

"Come in," Nita said. "Black was just leaving."

"Can't. I've got business downstairs."

Nita caught his arm. "Did you see Slade today?"

"Yes."

"Is he still alive?" Garrity demanded.

"Yes."

Garrity swore. "Then I was right, damn you. What do you think Cole's going to do when he hears?"

"Nothing. He said not to go hog wild. I didn't."

Womack turned again, and this time Nita let him go. She was still standing in the doorway, staring perplexedly after him, when he went down the stairs. If Garrity hadn't told her his suspicions, he would now, and in the morning Chapman would hear.

A dozen men were waiting in the lobby for him. As he came down the stairs, a fat bald man with a star on his shirt demanded, "What was the shooting about?"

"Who are you?"

"Jim Kelsey. I own the Mercantile next door, and I'm supposed to be the town marshal. You're thinking I'm a damned poor one, and maybe I am, but I'll tell you one thing: I don't cotton to the notion of having a gunslick like you hanging around this town."

"What are you gonna do about it?"

"Maybe nothing," Kelsey said truculently, "but if you get out of line, I will."

"It's somebody else who was out of line. A dry-gulcher was hiding across the street."

"You get him?"

"No." Womack pulled his gun, ejected the empties and reloaded. "Took you a long time to see what was going on."

"I ain't paid to get into no street fight," Kelsey muttered. "There's a stage leaving in the morning. You'd best be on it."

Womack looked down at the gun in his hand, then brought his gaze to the townsmen who stood behind the marshal. It was obvious that they sided with Jim Kelsey. They had no liking for the trouble that was shaping up on the mesa; they knew that in the long run they would be hurt if the combine won, but still they would not make a stand against the big outfits.

"The Piersons thought they'd make me take the stage before I got to Dogdance." Womack dropped his gun into leather and laid his gaze on Kelsey's fat face. "Joe Pierson's dead."

"I didn't say you *had* to be on it." Kelsey stared at the floor, the corners of his mouth working. "I just said it'd be best if you was."

Womack laughed softly. "I took a job here, Marshal, and I won't be on that stage till its done. Who runs this burg, you or Red Manion?"

"Neither one," the hotel clerk said wearily. "I'm getting pretty damned tired of trying to manage a business and know I've got to do this or that just to please Cole Chapman."

Kelsey's head lifted. "We're all in the same boat, Womack. If you're working for the combine like everybody says, you know how it is. We can't make you leave, but I want you to be damned sure you know you ain't welcome."

"That's right," another man said. "We're caught in the squeeze, and it's bad enough without a gunslick stranger horning in."

"You may be in more of a squeeze than you know," Womack said. "Slade's purty proddy. Suppose he rides into town with his neighbors? Maybe he'll take grub out of the stores and dinero out of Ryan's bank. He might even feel like burning you out. I ain't sure you can blame him. Push a man like Slade far enough, and you'll make a hell of a mean outlaw out of him."

"You ain't helping none," Kelsey said. "How much money would it take to get you to slope out of here?"

"You ain't got enough." Womack cocked his hat back, his eyes contemptuous. "Funny thing. No matter how tough the squeeze gets, there ain't a man among you who's got the guts it takes to do anything about it."

Pushing past Kelsey, Womack crossed the street to the Chinaman's and had his supper. Good enough food, he supposed, but it was tasteless to him. When he returned to the hotel, he found that everyone had left but the clerk, who eyed him with stony indifference. Womack got his key and climbed the stairs. He saw that the light under Nita's door was gone, and he wondered what the relationship was between her and Black Garrity.

He went into his room and locked the door behind him. As an extra precaution he shoved the chair under the knob. He did not light a lamp, for there was no shade on the window. Whoever had tried to kill him might try again. He went to bed, his gun under his pillow, and it was not until he lay on his back, his legs stretched out and his arms at his sides, that he realized how tired he was.

It was not so much weariness of body as it was weariness of spirit and mind. He was tired of the ceaseless vigilance, tired of little men like the townsmen who hated Cole Chapman but did nothing about it, tired of trying to figure out a pattern that was like so many others and yet so different. There was a moment of regret in him for taking the job Ed Hovey had offered. He'd have been smarter to have followed his nose just as he had planned; he should have got out of this country and gone to some place where he could have been just plain Bill Smith. Then the regret left him, and there, in the silence and the darkness, he faced his problem.

He could not cut away his past just by following his nose. The only way he could do so was to sit in the judgment seat; he had to give thought to what Rose Hovey called justice. A man had to change more than the purpose of his life: he had to change the things he did; he had to do something that would make amends for the old life.

The elements responsible for the change had been in him; but if he had followed his nose as he'd planned, the change would not have taken place. It had taken the week in Denver and the talks with Ed and Rose to do the job. Now, more important than anything else was the intense desire to do what Rose wanted him to. Whatever happened from here on, he would not have the regrets he would have had if he had gone on being the same Bill Womack he had been.

Any real change was an emotional revolution. He understood that. He just wasn't sure about himself. There were the yesterdays that had been lived and could not be changed. There had been no unrest then because the justice of what he was doing had not been a question in his mind. The writing on the book named Yesterday was indelible; but there was another book named Tomorrow. He had no idea of how many pages were in it, blank pages that he must write upon: one, perhaps hundreds. He might die tomorrow and he might live fifty years; but that wasn't important. What was important was whether he was capable of doing the kind of writing that Rose Hovey wanted him to do.

For a time he lay there, nurturing the thought of Rose and bringing the image of her trim, small body into his mind. Slowly the tension drained out of him. He thought of the differences between her and Ed and these other people; of the differences between their standards of living, their sense of values, their conceptions of justice. It was like comparing mountain peaks with a dry, sage-covered flat. There was nothing phony about Rose, and for that reason she would sense false standards in anyone else. He would never win her approval until he had honestly accepted her way of life. Even accepting was not enough. He must make her believe in him.

Then, almost asleep, a new thought brought him suddenly awake. The man who had tried to kill him tonight might have been Paddy Ryan. The old man had saved his life, he knew; he had found himself liking and trusting Ryan; he had even been tempted to

tell him the truth about why he had come to Dillon
Mesa. Still, long experience had taught him that often
the man he felt most like trusting was the man who
would shoot him in the back if the opportunity came
to him. There was no telling what motives had really
prompted Ryan to ride out to Ira Slade's Lazy S.
Before Womack finally dropped off to sleep, he had
accepted the hard fact that, for the moment, Paddy
Ryan was an enigma.

Chapter 8: Bow and Arrow

WOMACK LEFT TOWN EARLY THE NEXT MORNING, FORKING
the same livery horse he had ridden the day before.
Clouds had not cleared from the sky, and light was
slow to come to a dark wet world. It had rained hard
just before dawn, and now the smell of damp grass
and cedars was in the heavy air. Thunder still rolled
out of the sky from somewhere to the east of him. It
was the kind of dank cheerless day that Womack
hated, and he found himself hoping that the clouds
would break away and he could see the sun.

He passed a ranch an hour or so after he left town, a
big outfit with a rambling frame house and several
barns and outbuildings and a labyrinth of corrals. A
row of young cottonwoods grew in front of the house.
This, Womack knew, would be Chapman's CC.

Everything about the place gave the impression of
permanence. Chapman, Womack thought, was a man
who would never permit the possibility of failure to
enter his mind. He had built for eternity, for himself
and his children and his children's children. When he
had planted the cottonwoods he had doubtless
dreamed of the day when they would be giants and he

would sit in their shade, watching his grandchildren operate the ranch he had built from schemes and ruthless pressures and the spilled blood of others. Cole Chapman was a little man, therefore his dreams would be correspondingly big.

Womack had no desire to see Chapman now. He wanted to talk to Rose first, for there were questions that must be answered. When he had ridden in on the stage he had not known enough about local politics to ask questions, or to understand them even if Rose had given him the entire picture. She had known that, so she had not tried to tell him anything.

A mile or so past the CC, Womack came to a fork in the road. From the way Rose had described the country, he knew that the south fork would lead to Manion's Mallet Four and Lowrie's Slash Triangle. He continued east, climbing steadily now, the first foothills of the San Juan range rising directly in front of him.

Womack's thoughts turned to Abner Lowrie, the hawk-nosed smiling man who had not opened his mouth after Womack had walked into the combine meeting, the man Ira Slade had said was the only friend they had. That, Womack was certain, was wrong. A man who would sell his own side out was not capable of being a friend to anyone. Slade, made desperate by his position, would not question Lowrie's motives. He would reach for the first straw that might help him keep afloat.

It was midmorning when Womack came to Grant Hovey's Bow and Arrow. The contrast between it and Chapman's CC shocked Womack. There was a small log house, not more than four rooms at the most, with a huge stone fireplace along one end and a front porch that held a couple of weathered, rawhide-bottom chairs. A log barn stood to the north; there were some pole corrals and slab sheds behind it. A small stream roared down from the steep aspen-covered slope behind the buildings, slowed as it reached the level of the mesa, and ran on toward Devil River, flowing placidly here between the buildings and the base of the hill.

Womack had seen many ranches like the Bow and Arrow; it was the comparison with Chapman's CC that surprised him. Hovey's place had the appearance of a pioneer ranch. The buildings were those a man would put up when he first came to a country, temporary, made from the wood of the forest itself, the quickest and cheapest material that a man could lay his hands on. Rose had said her father was the first to come to the mesa, but in all the years since then he had apparently changed nothing.

The ranch, Womack thought, was a key to Grant Hovey's character. He hadn't gone ahead, improved, prospered; he had hung on, and that was all. Perhaps Chapman had been well fixed when he'd come; but whether he had or not, he had spread out and he'd made money. There was a sense of permanence about the CC; the Bow and Arrow had a transient quality, as if Grant Hovey was surprised each spring to find he was still in business.

Smoke rising from the chimney was the only sign of life about the place. Rose was probably in the house, Womack thought as he dismounted and tied; but before he could find out, he saw Grant Hovey come out of the barn, a bridle in his hand. They faced each other for a moment, Hovey staring in the surly way of a man who is instinctively suspicious of strangers. Womack wanted to see Rose, but he decided he had better talk to Hovey first.

"Howdy," Womack said, and walked toward Hovey.

"Howdy," the other replied in a cool, repellent tone.

Womack went on until he stood within five feet of Hovey. He stopped, eyes raking the Bow and Arrow owner. He was probably fifty, Womack judged, a heavy man given more to fat than muscle, with a round-cheeked face that held a network of purple veins and a pair of bloodshot blue eyes that frankly showed hostility. This was the Grant Hovey who had sired two fine children, the man Paddy Ryan had said wasn't "worth a damn."

"I came to see Rose," Womack said. "I met her on the stage."

"I figured you'd want to see her," Hovey said, his tone still hostile. "Come here."

Hovey swung around and walked into the barn. He tossed the bridle into a corner and sat down on a pile of oat sacks. Womack followed, smelling the strong nitrogen odor of the stables and seeing the high piles of manure. He thought, Hovey's lazy as well as no good.

Womack stood looking down at Hovey, and there was an uneasy silence between them. Then Hovey got up and walked to a back corner. He dug around in some straw, found a nearly empty whisky bottle, and brought it back.

"Have a drink," Hovey said, extending the bottle.

Womack shook his head. "No thanks. Don't go good with my business."

"Killing business," Hovey said, with wicked condemnation, and raising the bottle to his lips, drained it and tossed it back into the corner.

"You wasn't against killing business the other day in town," Womack said.

Hovey reached into his pocket for a pipe and tobacco sack, eyes wavering to Womack's face and away from it. "I don't bust into Cole's business." He paused, and then, emboldened by his drink, added: "I'll give it to you straight, Womack. A lot of men are scared of you. It's like when I was a kid in Texas. When I got ornery, Ma would scare the pants off me by saying that if I didn't behave, she'd give me to the Comanches."

Womack felt the tug of anger. Hovey was yellow

right down to his bootheels, but he thought he was
hiding it. Womack said: "You're trying to say you ain't
scared of me. That it?"

"You're as fast as hell with your cutter, or so they
say." Hovey dribbled tobacco into his pipe bowl, his
hands trembling so that more of it fell to the barn floor
than dropped into the bowl. "I'd be scared if I was
pulling a gun on you, but I ain't. I'm just telling you
that I ain't gonna have you coming around here
sparking Rose."

"Why?"

"She's a damned fine girl, that's why. She's straight,
Womack. She ain't nothing like that damned Nita
Chapman, who's got Cole eating his heart out. I ain't
gonna see Rose throw herself away on the likes of
you."

"What's the matter with me?"

Hovey packed the tobacco down, eyes lowered. "I
don't need to tell you. We're respectable. We make our
living by working. What are you? A gun slinger, a
hired killer, a drifter who'd make love to a girl and
leave her. You ain't gonna do it, mister, not to Rose.
I'll stop you if I have to use a scattergun on you."

The anger was close to the surface in Womack now,
so close that it was a struggle to keep his hands off
Hovey's fat neck. Respectable! The same damned
word he'd heard fifty times, the word that had been in
his mind in Denver and had been the cause of the
sourness that had plagued him, the word Paddy Ryan
had used in much the same way.

"So you're respectable," Womack said softly, "and
I'm not; but you was willing enough for the combine
to hire me to keep Ira Slade off your neck so you could
suck around after Cole Chapman when he was trying
to push honest men off their ranches. I don't want
your kind of respectability, mister, not any of it."

Hovey had fished a match out of his shirt pocket.
He held it in front of him, outraged eyes lifted to

Womack's angry face. "You can't talk to me that way. You'd best get out and earn the money the combine's paying you."

"I aim to see Rose first." Womack cuffed his hat back. "Hovey, there's something I've been wondering about. How could a no-good son like you have a pair of kids like Rose and Ed?"

Hovey seemed to collapse. He lowered his head, hands dropping to his knees. He said, "If you'd knowed their mother, you wouldn't ask."

It was an honest answer, and Womack lost the anger that had flamed in him. He sensed the shame that was in Hovey, and in spite of himself he felt some sympathy for the man.

"That's better," Womack said. "There's something else I want to know. Coming in on the stage, Rose said that when you was sober you hated Chapman and what he was doing. If that's true, why are you running around after him?"

"She shouldn't have said—"

"Is it true, or was Rose just wanting to think it was?"

"It's true enough, but it ain't no business—"

"I'm making it my business, Hovey. There's something fishy as hell about this range. I ain't the kind of hombre who takes my wages without asking some questions. I was out on the west end yesterday. Nothing out there that Chapman or any of the combine wants. Now what's it all about?"

Hovey motioned to the door. "Get out, Womack. Leave me alone."

The man was scared now, and he made no effort to hide it. His face was so pale that the purple veins stood out like dark splotches; his right hand shook as he tried to light the match he held. It broke in the middle, and he sat staring at it as if he did not know what to do with it.

"Rose would be proud of you," Womack said. "So would Ed."

"What do you know about Ed?"

"I met him in Denver. That's why I'm here."

Hovey lifted his head. "What do you mean by that?"

"Don't ask me. Answer my questions. I can't help you or Rose or Ed if I don't get the straight of things."

"Help me?" Hovey breathed. "What the hell! A gun slinger hired by Cole Chapman wouldn't help me. Get out and leave me alone."

"You need help, mister, and you need it damned bad. Look at who you're teamed up with. Chapman will throw you overboard the minute he don't need you; Manion's the kind who takes Chapman's orders because he likes to play big and Chapman got him the star; and Lowrie's trying to double-cross the lot of you. That's the kind of playmates you've got, Hovey."

"You're lying."

"No, I ain't. I could recite chapter and verse, but you're so muddleheaded you wouldn't see it. You'll let Chapman take you snipe hunting and you'll hold the sack. That's the kind of a fool you are. You ain't fit to have the kind of kids you've got."

"No," Hovey said miserably, "I ain't." He looked up, his pipe held in one hand, the broken match in the other. "Why are you talking this way?"

Womack hesitated, knowing that there was little value in holding back the truth. With Garrity guessing why he was here, Chapman would soon know regardless of what Hovey said or did.

"All right, Hovey, I'll tell you; but if you let it out to anyone I'll skin you. I'll skin you alive and hang your hide up to dry. Savvy?"

"Yeah, I savvy."

"All right. Ed looked me up in Denver and hired me to come here to keep you out of trouble, which same you're headed for as sure as the Lord made little apples. Rose waited for me in Colatas so she could talk to me. Ed paid me $1,000, and Rose is giving me another thousand when the job's done. That's how much they think of you, although I'm damned if I know why."

Hovey began to cry, not the crying of a drunken man, but that of one who has lost the courage to face this day and the days that lay ahead. Turning, Womack walked to the door. He rolled a smoke, eyes on the long steep slope of the hill behind the house. There was good summer graze up there, just as there was all around this country. Grant Hovey could have done well, as well as Chapman, if there had been any depth to him.

"Come here," Hovey said.

Womack swung around as Hovey wiped a sleeve across his face. "You want to talk to me?"

"Chapman will kill you when he finds out why you're here."

"That's my worry."

Hovey fished another match out of his pocket and fired his pipe. He pulled hard on it, as if trying to extract courage from it. Then he said: "I came here from the San Luis Valley. So did Chapman. We both had some money and some cattle. I wouldn't have left if I hadn't had to. I got into a jangle with a neighbor and killed him."

Hovey stopped and took the pipe out of his mouth. "I shot him in the back. Chapman knew about it. He showed up here after I did. Blackmailed me. I had to give him money and most of my beef for nothing. Since then I've jumped when he hollers." Hovey lifted his eyes defiantly. "Now you know, and you can turn me over to the law. Maybe that's why you're here."

"No," Womack said, "It's not. One more thing. Why is Chapman so bent on pushing the little fry off their places?"

"I don't know, Womack. I just don't know, but it's the way Chapman works. Before you came to the meeting, he was talking about throwing our crews together and cleaning Slade and his bunch out. I was supposed to lead 'em. He was going to the mining camps up Devil River to wind up the deal for the beef we've got to sell."

"Then when I showed up, he was willing for me to do the job?"

"That's right. He's always willing to let somebody else take the risks."

"I'm going in to see Rose."

Hovey got up. "Let her alone, Womack. If I have to, I'll get down on my knees and beg. She ain't for you, I tell you."

Womack stared at the man, hating him and despising him, yet bound to help him. He said, "I need to talk to Rose." Turning, he walked to the house, remembering that Hovey had admitted he'd shot a man in the back. And Grant Hovey was a man who could claim respectability.

Womack knocked on the front door. Hovey was standing in front of the barn staring at him, and suddenly it occurred to Womack that Grant Hovey could have been the man who had shot at him the night before in Dogdance. Shooting at a man from the darkness of a weed-covered lot would be Hovey's size. If Rose had spoken well of him to her father, Hovey might have been prompted by the fear that Rose would fall in love with him. Then Womack dismissed the thought, for it was wishful thinking. He had no real hope that Rose would speak well of him.

She opened the door, smiling. "Good morning, Mr. Womack. I was hoping you'd come in. I saw you ride up a little while ago."

He touched his hat brim, suddenly embarrassed for no reason except that he wanted this girl to like him, and he knew that everything in his past was against him.

She was wearing a dark apron over a blue-flowered house dress, and her sleeves were rolled up above the elbows of her strong arms; her auburn hair was just a little untidy, and there was a smudge of flour on one cheek; but her appearance did not seem to give her concern.

"I'd like to talk to you—" he began.

"Well, then, come in." She stepped aside. "I want to talk to you, too. If I'm any judge of you and the way things are on the mesa, you've found out a good deal and you've probably got some questions I can't answer."

"I've found out some things, all right," he said, "and I've got some questions I hope you can answer."

He followed her across the living room. It was neat and clean but sparsely furnished with a few rawhide-bottom chairs, a worn horsehair sofa, and a pine table that held an assortment of tattered magazines and catalogues. A picture of a handsome young woman hung in an ornate gilt frame on the wall above the cavernous fireplace. Rose's mother, he thought, and wondered if Grant Hovey would have been different from what he was now if she had lived.

"Walk easy," Rose cautioned. "I've got a cake in the oven."

He followed her into the kitchen, feeling the heat from the range and smelling the rich fragrance of the baking cake. On the table was a dish of icing that she had been beating. She picked it up and set to work again, her spoon making a steady whisper of sound in the thick icing.

Suddenly aware that he was still standing, she said, "Sit down, Bill."

"I'm afraid to breathe," he said.

She laughed and nodded at a chair across the table from him. "My cake isn't that delicate. Sit down and ask the first question."

He tiptoed to the chair and sat down, holding his hat awkwardly in front of him. For a moment he was silent, content to look at her. Again she gave him the same impression of frank and open honesty that she had given when he sat beside her in the stage. She lacked the subtleties that so many women had, the roundabout ways of getting at the things they wanted.

Rose put her dish down, removed the cake from the oven, ran a knife blade around the rim of the pan, and upset the cake into a plate. She began icing it, working with quick deft strokes. When he still remained silent, she gave him a questioning look, as if wondering what had happened to his power of speech. At last she put her hands on her hips and looked intently at him.

"When I was a girl and wanted to say something and couldn't, my mother used to ask me if the cat had my tongue. Now I'm wondering that about you."

"I reckon that's it." He reached for tobacco and paper and then lowered his hand. "Too much to ask, maybe. I don't know where to start."

"Go ahead and smoke." She dropped into a chair across the table from him, a smile curving the corners of her mouth. "You're like Ed: can't talk without a cigarette in your mouth. You're a victim of habit, Mr. Womack."

He grinned wryly and began rolling a smoke. "I guess that's right. Well, the big question takes a woman to answer. What about Nita Chapman?"

The question wiped the smile from her lips. For a moment she regarded him gravely, and he sensed the sudden deep bitterness which rose in her. She was not, he thought, the kind of woman who would let her soul be corroded by hatred, yet now he had the distinct feeling that she hated Nita Chapman as she hated no other human being.

"An interesting question," she said at last. "What do you think about Nita?"

"I don't know." He sealed his cigarette and slipped it into his mouth. "I mean, I don't trust her; but it takes a woman to see through a woman. If it was a man, I'd trust my own judgment; but she ain't nothing like a man."

"If I told you what I think, you wouldn't believe me. Even if I told you what I've seen, you wouldn't believe me."

"I'd believe anything you say." He fired his cigarette, watching her closely. "Fact is, you're the only one on this range I'm sure I can believe."

"She came here three years ago," Rose said, "and took two rooms in the hotel. None of the women in town accepted her, but that didn't bother the men. Abner Lowrie and Cole both started courting her. She dangled one and then the other, and wound up marrying Cole."

"And maybe Chapman did some changing about then."

Rose nodded. "That's right. He's always been the kind of man who wanted to be big. He owned a piece of Paddy Ryan's bank and he'd bought a share of Jim Kelsey's store, but after he married Nita he began acting twice as big."

"How?"

"Well, he got Red Manion elected sheriff. I don't know how, but I'll bet anything it was crooked. He lined up the mining-camp market for the combine, and he promised the others that if they'd go along he'd make them rich. Lately he's been putting pressure on Ira Slade and his neighbors. He even brought in another herd from the Dolores country so he could claim he needed more range. Actually, there's more grass on this side of the mesa than he'll ever use."

"Then the trouble really goes back to the time when he got married?"

"That's right. I think everything can be laid on Nita, but I can't prove it and it wouldn't do any good if I could." She glanced at the clock on the shelf above the stove. "It's half past ten. Have you got time to take a ride with me?"

"Sure."

She rose. "Was Nita in town when you left?"

"She was last night. Dunno about this morning."

"There's a good chance I can show you something that might explain the whole business. You see, I ride a lot just to be riding. That's why I see things that no one else does. The men don't go chasing around unless they're after cattle or something, so I think I know what goes on better than any man on the mesa."

"If you think I wouldn't believe—"

"I'd rather have you see it. Then you'll know it just isn't my imagination or evil mind." She hesitated, biting her lip, then said, "Bill, we've had our share of bad men on this range, men like the Piersons; but a dozen bad men can't make the trouble one bad woman can, and I believe Nita's just plain bad."

He rose. "Want me to saddle your horse?"

"I wish you would. I'll change my clothes and fix a lunch. My horse is the sorrel gelding. Dad will help you if he's out there."

"I reckon I won't need any help." He moved to the back door and then turned. "Your dad don't want me seeing you."

She frowned. "I'm almost twenty-one. That's something Dad never seems to remember."

Womack shifted uneasily. "I told him why I was here."

"You shouldn't have done—" she began angrily, then caught herself. "Why?"

"Garrity's guessed. He's bound to tell Chapman sooner or later. I figured your dad couldn't do no harm if he knew, and it might do some good. He was pretty hostile when I rode up."

"I know," she said. "He's like that sometimes. I wish you hadn't, but it's too late now."

He went out then, and when he reached the barn he found that Grant Hovey had gone. Probably to tell Chapman, Womack thought, and felt the stir of anger in him. Paddy Ryan had made a great understatement when he'd said that Hovey was no good. Still,

Womack had learned long ago that good and evil are never absolute. It was possible that Grant Hovey honestly thought he was protecting Rose by securing Chapman's help in ridding Dillon Mesa of Bill Womack.

Chapter 9: Love Affair

WOMACK DID NOT WAIT LONG IN FRONT OF THE HOUSE WITH the horses before Rose came out with a flour sack of food in one hand. She had changed to a man's shirt and levis and riding boots. Quickly she tied the sack behind the saddle and stepped up, ignoring Womack's hand. He swung aboard, thinking that Rose was the kind of woman who would never lean upon a man. She'd carry her own weight no matter how heavy the burden was.

Rose headed directly south, giving no explanation of what she intended doing or what she expected him to see. They followed cattle trails through the scrub oak, and half an hour from the time they left Bow and Arrow they reined up on the north rim of a steep-walled canyon.

"North fork of Cedar Creek," she told him. "It meets the south fork four or five miles west of here, and the main stream runs into Ute Creek above Dogdance a piece."

"What's the creek that goes by your place?"

"Bear Creek. It runs into Ute Creek about two miles above town. I told you there was plenty of water here. The west end of the mesa was dry, but it isn't any problem here."

He nodded thoughtfully. "You've got enough to

farm half the mesa if these creeks were dammed and a ditch system put in."

She gave him a sharp look. "I thought you'd always worked for cattlemen?"

"I have, mostly. Why?"

"Then I should think you'd talk like a cattleman. Farming the mesa is the last thing any of us would think of. There are a few farms on Ute Creek below town, and that's all there are on the mesa."

He grinned. "I ain't intending to put in no irrigation system, if that's what you're worrying about."

"No, I wasn't worrying about it. Guns and plows don't go together."

He looked down into the canyon at the chain of pools made by a series of beaver dams. He said somberly: "Don't make the mistake most folks do, Rose. Just because I've favored guns in the past is no sign I'm going to keep on favoring 'em."

"Does a man ever change?"

"He might if he gets sick of his life." He rolled a smoke, searching for words. "Some men start off doing what they want to do, and they keep on doing it. Or some get into a rut and never climb out. Me, I just drifted for a while. Didn't much like to work after my folks died, and a farmer back in Missouri took me and tried to get two men's work out of me. I ran away and sort of built up to what I am, and I ain't proud of it."

"You don't even like it, do you?"

"No. Fact is, I never did." He fired his cigarette. "No future but a slug from some fool kid who wants to make a name for himself. Or getting drilled in a range war that don't make no never mind to me either way." He glanced at her again, wondering if she understood what he was trying to say. "This is my last job. I came pretty close to not taking this one."

"Why did you?"

"Money. Where else could I make $2,000 as quick as this?"

"I see," she breathed. "And what will you do with the money?"

"Buy a ranch. I've got a little outfit in mind in South Park that can be bought cheap. Trouble is, somebody may beat me to it."

"Ranching means work," she said.

"Sure, but working on a Missouri farm for a mean old goat is one thing. Working for myself is something else. I aim to take a crack at it. Your $2,000 with what I've got will give me a start and little bit to go on."

For a moment she stared at him, frankly surprised by what he had said. Then she asked, "Why did you say what you did about farming on Dillon Mesa?"

"Well, when you follow my business, you find out there's usually a pattern to trouble. I've been in half a dozen states and territories and on all kinds of ranges. They're different. You know, the grass and rocks and brush, the climate and such; but people are pretty much the same. There are just a few things that make 'em tick, and you get so you look for them things. Somebody wants a piece of range that another man claims, or maybe it's a water hole. And then there's times when a man just gets afraid, or hates somebody so much he wants him out of the way."

"This is different?"

"Sure it's different. Don't follow no pattern. Like I told you before, you and Ed are trying to stop trouble instead of make it. You talk about justice, which same is a word I'm plumb unfamiliar with. And this business of the combine going after grass they don't need and which ain't no good just don't look bright."

"You think somebody is stirring things up to get the mesa so he can put water on it and sell it to settlers? That sounds pretty farfetched to me."

Womack shrugged. "Maybe so. I said this don't follow the pattern. I was just wondering why."

She was silent, thinking about it. "There isn't anybody here who could do it. Paddy Ryan has some money, but not enough. He isn't that kind anyhow, and nobody else has any money but Chapman."

He thought of telling her what Ryan had said about Abner Lowrie, then decided against it. He said: "Crazy notion, all right. I was just daydreaming."

"We'd better get along," she said. "This may be a wild-goose chase, but if it isn't there's no sense sitting here until it's too late."

She angled down the side of the canyon, reached the bottom, and followed the stream for a time, then crossed between two beaver dams and took up the opposite side. Womack followed, curiosity gnawing at him, but he refused to ask questions.

The sky had cleared, and the sun, almost noon-high, was hot and bright upon the wet earth. The scrub-oak leaves were turning scarlet, a sure sign that summer was behind them. This, Womack thought, might be the last warm day. When winter came to the high country, it came with a rush. The first snow would bring the cattle down from Angel Peak, and the combine would start the drive for the mining camps.

They angled southwest, an open country with grass knee-high on the horses. Ranch buildings showed to the left. Womack motioned toward them, asking, "Which outfit is that?"

"Mallet Four," Rose told him. "Red Manion's place. He's got a wife and two kids at home, but he doesn't spend much time with them. He's probably with the crew on Angel Peak. When Chapman's up to something, he sends Red out of the country so it'll be handy for him to overlook what goes on."

"Big outfit?"

"Biggest on the mesa except for Chapman's CC. He keeps three riders. Lowrie has one. We have a couple besides Ed. Dad doesn't ride much any more, but Ed will be back from Denver in time to help with the drive up Devil River."

"Lowrie's outfit is the smallest?"

She nodded. "He's just got a shirttailful of cows. I doubt if he'll have fifty steers to send up the river this fall."

"Ryan said his dad used to be the big fellow hereabouts."

"That's right. It was after he got dry-gulched that Chapman started running things." They reached a road that ran toward the Mallet Four buildings. Rose reined up and studied the soft earth for a moment. "Nobody's been along here since the rain. I suppose Red went up the creek to the cow camp instead of coming home. This way would be longer."

"Lowrie lives alone?"

"Through the summer. What he does to keep busy is anybody's guess, but one thing's sure: he doesn't work."

They went on across the road, and a moment later were lost in a forest of piñon and cedar. The land was lifting now, and they pulled down to a slower pace, then swung off the trail and cut directly to the left. Within a few minutes they reached another canyon.

"South fork of Cedar Creek," she said, and reining up, dismounted. "This is where we sit and spy. I hope we have something to spy on."

She took the flour sack down from behind her saddle and motioned with her head for Womack to follow. He obeyed, leaving the horses ground-hitched. A few pines were scattered about, and Rose paused beside one, dropping her sack at the base of the tree. She waited until he caught up with her, then dropped to her hands and knees and crawled to the rim.

"We're lucky," she said. "Take a look, but don't let him see you."

Womack followed. He lay belly-flat beside the girl and looked down into the canyon. Abner Lowrie was sitting beside the creek idly tossing rocks into a clear pool below a big beaver dam. There was a grassy bench above him under the opposite canyon wall. His horse was grazing there, fifty feet or so from Lowrie.

Womack drew back. "What does that prove?"

"Nothing yet." Opening the sack, she took out a beef sandwich and handed it to him. "This isn't much of a meal, but I didn't want to take time to fix any more."

"It's fine," he said.

There were more sandwiches and two pieces of cake that she had wrapped in paper. She shook her head in disgust when she opened the package and held it out to him.

"More crumbs than anything else," she said. "I knew that would happen."

"Don't hurt the taste," he said, filling his mouth with cake and licking the icing from a finger.

"I'm the best cook on the mesa." She spoke as if she were merely stating a fact that was beyond argument. "Someday after Ed gets back I'll cook a meal for all of us to prove it."

"I ain't augering." He gathered a handful of cake crumbs and crammed his mouth with them. "Not a bit."

Rose crawled to the rim and came back. "Still there."

Irritation stirred in Womack. "Why can't you just tell me—"

"You're here now," she said sharply. "You can wait a little longer."

He grinned. "Reckon I can. What about Paddy Ryan? Can you depend on what he says?"

"He's one of the few men in Dogdance you can count on," she said warmly. "He's like you, kind of sour on life, or the life he's been living, anyhow. He hates Chapman, but he goes along because there isn't much he can do by himself." She wadded up the paper and stuffed it into the sack. "Have you talked to Paddy?"

Womack nodded. "He said there was something kind of funny about what happened to Lowrie's outfit. Said he lost most of his cattle to Chapman."

"Or sold them. They're the only ones who know just what did happen. It wasn't long after old Jake Lowrie died that Chapman took most of the Slash Triangle cattle, and all but one of Lowrie's crew went to work for him. Chapman said he bought the cattle, and maybe he did." She drummed her fingers on a pine root, frowning. "You've seen Abner?"

"Yeah, just seen him, but I haven't heard him talk much. He was at the meeting, but he didn't open his mug all the time he was there."

"He's like that. Listens but doesn't say much. Funny thing. He's been on the mesa about as long as any of us, and longer than Chapman; but we all know what Chapman's like, and we don't know Abner."

"He ain't like his dad?"

"Not a bit. Old Jake was greedy and overbearing, and he looked just like you think a big cattle baron ought to look; but Abner's different. You wouldn't know he was Jake's boy."

"Ryan said he'd been away to school."

She nodded. "He was at Fort Collins for a while. That may be part of it, but he was kind of queer before. Bashful, maybe. Didn't go with girls or attend dances. Jake tried to make him, but he wouldn't go; or if he did, he'd just stand around and watch. He wasn't any better when he got back from school. And he won't work except when they cut out the steers to drive to the mining camps."

Rose crawled to the rim. She called softly, "Come here, Bill."

He moved to her and lay looking down into the canyon, bellyflat. A rider was coming up the creek. Lowrie was on his feet waving a hand. A moment later the rider swung around a patch of willows and came into the open. It was Nita Chapman.

"Well, I'll be damned," Womack breathed.

"I thought you would," Rose said. "It's like I said. Nobody would believe this unless they saw it."

The woman reined up beside Lowrie, and dismounted, and went into his arms. There was a long, passionate embrace, then she moved back from Lowrie and raised her hands to his cheeks. She said something, and Lowrie laughed and kissed her again.

Spying went against Womack's grain, and now he felt a little guilty. He glanced at Rose, who met his eyes, frowning. She said: "I know how you feel: sort of unclean, and you're wishing you hadn't come. You probably hate me for bringing you here."

"No, but—"

"Don't say it, Bill. I know it's wrong, but I think it's important. I doubt that Chapman knows. He's crazy about Nita, but I think he feels that something's wrong." She spread her hands. "I always have the feeling that Chapman has to be big and important so people won't notice what he looks like." She motioned toward the couple in the bottom of the canyon. "Maybe he thinks he can hold Nita by getting bigger and more important."

Womack had had much the same idea. He nodded, thinking of how Chapman had briefly bared his soul in the back room of the Starlight, how he had needlessly humiliated Nita in her hotel room. The explanation, Womack thought, might lie in his fear that he was losing his wife; perhaps he was striking back to hurt her as she was hurting him. Womack remembered, too, what Black Garrity had said about Chapman losing Nita. Perhaps Garrity was aware of this relationship between Nita and Abner Lowrie.

"I think you've hit on something," Womack said finally, "but I ain't sure it'll do us any good."

"I think it will before we're done," the girl said. "At least it might help explain what you said about this range not having the usual pattern."

Nita was sitting down on the bank now, her legs under her, and Lowrie lay with his head on her lap. They were talking earnestly, but the distance was too great to catch even a whisper of sound. Suddenly Lowrie sat up and pounded a fist into a palm, shouting something. Nita shook her head and pulled him back to her lap.

"We've seen enough," Womack said, and crawled back from the rim.

Rose followed, watching him. She said, "What will you do now?"

"Dunno. My job was to keep your dad out of trouble, which same I doubt that I can. Looks to me like he's in mighty close with Chapman."

Rose's lips tightened. "And he'll do what Chapman says unless you can stop him, and that takes you to Chapman."

Womack cuffed back his hat and scratched his head. "Old man Lowrie was shot after Abner got back from school. That right?"

"That's right, about two weeks after Abner got home. One of the Slash Triangle hands who signed on with Chapman said they'd quarreled just before old Jake was killed. Abner didn't want to stay home and work, and Jake said he was going to whether he wanted to or not."

"Didn't anybody ever add that up?"

She nodded. "I guess we all had the same idea, but there was never any proof. After all, you can't arrest a man for killing his father unless there is some proof."

They mounted and rode back the way they had come. Womack said, "How'd you happen to stumble on this place in the first place?"

"It was just an accident. I told you I rode a lot. It was one afternoon last spring, kind of hot, and I got sleepy. I took a nap just about where we were, and when I woke up they were down there. I've seen them several times since then, usually after she's stayed in town for a while."

He told her what had happened at Slade's place and about Lowrie being there. Then he asked, "How do you add that up?"

"I add it up like I do everything else about Abner

Lowrie. He strings along with Chapman because he can't fight Chapman alone, but he thinks he can with Slade and the others. When a man wants another man's wife, he'll do anything to fix it so he can have her. Isn't that right?"

"I reckon so," Womack agreed; "but suppose Chapman cashed in and Nita married Lowrie. That wouldn't really change anything on the mesa except get your dad's nose out of a mousetrap."

"It would change everything, Bill. Lowrie and Nita would sell and go away. The rest of us could get along."

"Looks like she wished she'd married Lowrie in the first place."

"Maybe, or maybe they had this idea all the time; I don't know. But I still think Nita is the cause of our trouble."

They reached a narrow road running north and south through the piñons. Womack reined up, asking, "Where does this go, Lowrie's place?"

She nodded. "It's about a mile or so on the other side of the south fork of Cedar Creek." She frowned. "Now what have you got in your head?"

"I aim to have a talk with Lowrie."

"That's crazy, Bill. If he had any idea that you'd seen what you just have, he'd kill you."

"He'd try, I reckon, but I ain't sure I'll tell him. Mostly I want to know why he left me tied up in Slade's house yesterday. He knew I was there."

She gripped the saddle horn, dark blue eyes frankly worried. She said, "When you hire a gunman like Ed and I have done, I guess you aren't supposed to think about his life."

A quick smile cut the grimness from his face. "That's right. All you lose is your money. My life is my risk."

"But I'm not made that way, Bill. I didn't really think how it would be when I had the crazy idea of bringing you here. I thought you could bluff Chapman, or just break him and Dad up."

"Nobody bluffs Cole Chapman. If I'm sizing this up right, he's a little crazy, and a crazy man is the worst kind of a man to buck. But this other business of breaking your dad and Chapman up is something else. I think it can be done."

She was silent a moment, eyes searching his lean, weathered face. Then she said: "I'm not like the kind of people who have hired you. I'd never forgive myself if you were killed."

"I don't aim to be killed. I told you this was my last job. Remember?"

"That's exactly what I'm remembering. Come on back with me, Bill. I think you ought to talk to Dad some more."

"I'll see you tonight. Right now I've got to talk with Lowrie."

She threw out a hand in a weary gesture. "Someday I want to meet a man who isn't stubborn."

"You wouldn't like him."

"Maybe not. Bill, you haven't thought how this will be. You're going to make enemies of almost everybody on the mesa. If Chapman turns on you—which he will when he finds out why you're here—you'll have the law against you, and Red Manion will frame you for something."

"I've thought of that, but real friends don't change. I'm hoping you and Ed never will."

"But that won't help you—"

"I'll see you tonight," he said, and reined away.

Chapter 10: Bullet in the Back

WITHIN FIFTEEN MINUTES FROM THE TIME WOMACK LEFT Rose, he reached the south fork of Cedar Creek and rode down the twisting trail into the canyon. He paused at the bottom to let his horse drink, and went on up the south side, his mount laboring in the mud. Clouds had moved in from the high San Juan range, momentarily covering the sun and then drifting away from it, so that the earth was touched by alternate patches of shadow and sunlight.

Womack topped the rim and reined up to let his horse blow. The land lifted ahead of him, the road a narrow lane between the aspens. In the high altitude their leaves had begun to fall, forming a sodden mass that muffled his horse's hoofs. He went on, climbing steadily, and the clouds, thick and black now, made an overcast that covered the sun. A cold damp wind rushed down the mountainside. It would rain before night, Womack thought. There might even be snow, and he wondered if they had begun the drive from Angel Peak to the lower altitude of the mesa.

It was still early in the afternoon when he reached Lowrie's Slash Triangle. The ranch looked exactly as he had pictured it, a sort of ghost spread that had long ago lost its glory. The house was a sprawling log structure; the barns and outbuildings, too, were constructed of logs, and to the west there was a maze of pole corrals, empty except for half a dozen horses.

All of it showed the weathering of sun and wind and rain, and everywhere there was an air of emptiness. Some of the windows of the house were boarded up,

most of the doors of the outbuildings hung askew
from broken hinges, and several of the corrals needed
repair. In one sweeping look Womack saw enough
work to keep a man busy for weeks. Either Abner
Lowrie was lazy, as Rose seemed to think, or he did
not plan to stay here.

"Hello the house," Womack called.

There was no answer except the echo of Womack's
words. He sat his saddle a moment, listening to the
steady murmur of Ute Creek in the trough to the
south, to the wind whistling down through the spruce
trees on the side of the mountain above him. It
seemed to Womack that a weird, depressing atmos-
phere of ruin lay upon this ranch, and it struck him as
queer that Abner Lowrie or any man should live here.

Womack had no idea when Lowrie would be back,
but with another storm threatening he did not think it
would be long. Lowrie would not keep Nita out in it,
and he certainly would not bring her here.

Womack rode around the barn and dismounted. He
hunkered there out of the wind, smoking; and without
conscious direction his thoughts turned to Rose. He
wondered why she had been concerned about his
safety. Probably she did not want to be responsible for
his life. She was the kind of person who would never
feel right if she was the cause of a man's death,
directly or indirectly; but he could not dislodge the
hope that there was more to her concern than that. For
the first time in his life Womack found himself
thinking of his future as a man does who wants to
build something, a future that would be entirely
different from his past. As far as his thinking was
concerned, the break with his past was complete, the
same sort of break that Paddy Ryan had made when
he had become a banker.

Now, foolish or not, Womack could not separate
Rose from his future. That, too, was different from the
thinking he had done in the past. Then a sourness
began working through him, his mind turning to what

Grant Hovey had said. The man had called him a gun
slinger, a hired killer, a drifter who would make love
to a girl and leave her. Probably they all thought the
same thing. Even Rose. He knew, and the knowledge
added to his bitterness, that he could not ask a girl like
Rose to marry him, not until he had become something more than the things Grant Hovey had called
him.

Womack was not aware of Abner Lowrie's approach
until the man had ridden into the yard and stripped
his horse. Apparently he had not noticed any fresh
tracks in the road or yard, for he started toward the
house, his head down against the wind.

Womack called, "Lowrie." The wind whipped the
word downslope, and the man, not hearing, went on.
Womack called again, shouting this time, "Lowrie!"

Startled, the Slash Triangle owner wheeled, a hand
moving downward toward his gun. Then he saw who
it was, and he froze, fingers wrapped around the cedar
butt of his .45.

"You aiming to draw, Lowrie?" Womack asked,
coming on until he was within five feet of the man.

Lowrie grinned. "Not after I saw who you were.
What are you doing up here?"

"Wanted to see you."

Curiosity stirred the man's hawk-nosed face.
"That's funny. Thought you went after Slade."

Womack discovered one thing in that brief moment: Lowrie had the kind of poker face that could
hide surprise or fear or any other emotion that was in
him. Now he seemed amused, as if Womack's presence was of no real concern to him.

"I went to see Slade," Womack corrected him.

"Well, come on in. Cold enough today to freeze the
ears off a brass monkey. I'll build a fire and get you a
drink."

"I'll stay out here." Womack motioned toward
Lowrie's gun. "You were going to pull. Who did you
think I was?"

Lowrie shrugged. "Hard to tell. This is a tough country, in case you hadn't found out."

"Who's gunning for you? Chapman? Or Garrity, maybe?"

The aloof, indifferent manner did not change. "Hell, no," Lowrie said. "A man's friends don't go gunning for him. I just didn't know."

"A man shot at me when I got back to town," Womack said. "It was pretty late. After dark. Were you in town?"

"I didn't take a shot at you, if that's what you're getting at." Lowrie seemed shocked by the thought. "You must take me for a fool. I'm no gun slinger. Anyhow, why should I?"

"I had a notion you didn't go along with Chapman in his idea of clearing the west end of the mesa."

"I'll go along because it's what Cole wants. Makes me no never mind either way. I've got all the range I need." He swept a hand out in a wide, inclusive motion. "Hell, you can see for yourself. I'm keeping afloat, and that's all."

"I thought the combine was made up of big boys."

Lowrie laughed derisively. "Not by a damned sight. Ira Slade runs more stock than I do. Let's put it this way, Womack. The combine is made up of men who are under Cole's thumb. You probably saw that. When he calls a meeting, he tells us what we're gonna do. He don't bother to ask what we think. We don't try telling him, neither. It's easier to get along that way."

That, Womack thought, was certainly true, but it didn't answer the questions that were in his mind. He let Lowrie have it then, asking, "Why didn't you get me out of Slade's house yesterday when he told you he had me inside?"

Still Lowrie's expression did not change. He said flatly: "You're loco. I ain't seen Slade for weeks, and I ain't been within ten miles of his place for longer than that. Ain't healthy for any of us out there." He scratched his beaky nose, scowling. "Just what are you driving at, Womack?"

"I don't usually call a man a liar, but I'm calling you one. You rode up just after Mrs. Slade cracked me with a frying pan and Slade tied me up. They aimed to hang me for Chapman to look at. You said that'd give Manion a chance to move in and they'd better go after Chapman."

"You've got me between a rock and the hard place. I don't cotton to being called a liar, but if I call you one you'll pull your iron. If half the tales they tell about you are true, I wouldn't have a chance."

"I'm asking questions because I don't savvy the way the land lays around here," Womack said. "Slade didn't hang me because Paddy Ryan saved my hide, but I talked to Slade before I left. He said you were the only friend they had on this side of the mesa."

"Well, sir, he was sure fooling himself. When I buck Cole Chapman, I'll be a lot crazier than I am right now."

This, Womack saw, wasn't getting him anywhere. He could stand here till dark, and Lowrie wouldn't give anything away he didn't want to. Womack thought of telling him what he and Rose had seen that morning, but decided against it. He would gain nothing except a bullet in the back if Lowrie had the opportunity to give him one without endangering himself.

"All right," Womack said, "but I aim to tell Chapman he's getting double-crossed."

"He won't believe you," Lowrie said with cool confidence. "He's known me for years, and he's mighty sure I don't have the guts to double-cross him. You don't know your boss very well, Womack."

"Maybe not."

"I'm freezing. If you want to talk, come on inside."

"Thanks," Womack said, "but I reckon I'll slope along."

Lowrie wheeled and went on to the house. Womack
waited, wondering if the man would turn and make a
try for his gun, but apparently the thought was not in
Lowrie's mind. When the door slammed, Womack ran
toward his horse. He reached the corner of the barn
and stood there out of the wind, still uncertain of the
man's intentions. When he saw that Lowrie was
content to let it go, he mounted, and making a circle
of the corrals, swung into the road a quarter of a mile
downslope.

It started to rain after he crossed the south fork of
Cedar Creek. Stopping, he put on his slicker and then
went on, his thoughts on Abner Lowrie. Even now he
could not make an absolute judgment of the man, and
he could understand why nobody seemed to know
him. Lowrie was the most capable liar Womack had
ever met; he could play any role he chose and play it
well, donning the expression that fitted the part as
easily as a woman puts on a dress to suit an occasion.
Womack wondered about Nita, wondered whether
she and Lowrie trusted each other or whether this was
a game that each was playing for the profit that could
be gained. Probably they were the only ones who knew
except Black Garrity, and he was not a man who
would talk until it suited him.

The rain slacked off before Womack reached the
road that ran past the CC and into town, but the sky
was dark and forbidding, and dusk was at hand,
hastened by the sullen clouds. He thought of going to
Chapman's ranch. He had to report to Chapman
sooner or later; and if Grant Hovey had gone to
Chapman that morning, he wanted to know what he
had said.

Womack hesitated. There was Paddy Ryan's part in
this to consider, and there was Black Garrity. It would
not be long until Chapman would find out that
Womack had no intention of pressing Slade and his
neighbors; he was bound to discover Womack's real
reason for coming here. Perhaps he already knew.

There was a question of timing, but he had promised to see Rose tonight. Chapman could wait.

Reluctantly Womack turned eastward toward the Bow and Arrow. A few flakes of wet snow were in the air as he jogged along, but he gave them scant attention. There was always a limit to what any one man could do, and for the first time in years he found himself wondering if he could accomplish what he had been hired for.

Womack balanced in his mind the allies he could count on against his potential enemies: Rose, Ed Grant, when the boy got back from Denver; possibly Paddy Ryan. He had been suspicious of the old banker last night, but Rose's feeling about him had changed that. Three of them, no more: a girl, a boy who wasn't here, and an old man who hated himself for bowing to Chapman but who lacked the courage to make a stand. Womack smiled grimly. Not much help against Chapman and Manion and Lowrie, probably against Garrity and most of the townsmen, and certainly against Ira Slade and his neighbors, unless they could be convinced he was not against them.

He was a traitor to God and man, Rose had said, if he used his talent to kill a man because someone ordered him to, and if he never gave the justice of it any thought. Well, he'd been a traitor to God and man many times, if Rose was right. Now, to please her, he was thinking of justice, he was risking his life by sitting in the judgment seat, and for what?

He shivered, wishing he had bought a sheepskin or Mackinaw before he'd left Dogdance. But the chill that passed through him did not come entirely from the cold. A sardonic grin touched his lips. He was Bill Womack, the man people thought was never afraid of anything. Well, he had a right to be afraid. Rose had said he'd wind up making enemies of almost everyone on the mesa, and it would probably work that way. Before, he had always been on the side that held the margin of power. Whatever law there had been had backed him. This was different, and because it was different, there was a challenge in it that he had never faced before, a challenge and a sense of satisfaction that came from knowing that he was giving some thought to the abstract principle of justice. There was satisfaction, too, in knowing he was on Rose Hovey's side.

It was almost dark when he glimpsed the lamplight in the Bow and Arrow ranchouse through the shifting snow flakes. An instant later his horse shied violently, so unexpectedly that it almost threw him. Womack pulled up, holding his horse under a tight rein, his eyes sweeping the opposite side of the road. In the thin dying light he saw the vague bulk of a man's body, motionless under a thin blanket of snow.

Womack dismounted and knelt beside the man. It was Grant Hovey, shot through the chest; and though he was very cold he was still alive, but that was all. If he didn't die from the wound, he'd probably die from exposure. With that thought, a sense of failure washed through Bill Womack. He had been hired to keep Grant Hovey out of trouble, but he had not been able to keep him from being shot.

Chapter 11: Shuffle and Deal

WOMACK LIFTED HOVEY'S LIMP BODY INTO THE SADDLE, and stepping up behind him, rode into the clearing that held the Bow and Arrow buildings. There was a lantern in the barn, the light shining through the open door, and Womack called, "Rose."

She came out of the barn at once and walked toward him, holding the lantern high as she asked, "What is it, Bill?"

"Your dad. He's shot."

He heard the sharp intake of her breath. "Is he alive?"

"He's alive, but that's all you can say for him."

Womack was on the ground now, and when she reached him he saw that she was wearing a wool scarf around her head and a heavy coat. She said: "I went out to take care of the horses and found his bay. I don't know how long he'd been there. I was starting to look for Dad."

Womack lifted Hovey's limp body from the saddle and carried him to the house. Opening the door for him, Rose motioned to a bedroom on his left. "In there." Womack laid him on the bed, Rose bringing a lamp from the front room and placing it on the ancient scarred bureau.

"He needs a doctor," Womack said. "Needs one bad."

"There isn't a doctor in the county," she told him. "The closest is in Montrose or the mining camps up Devil River."

Womack removed Hovey's coat, seeing that the wound was not as bad as he had supposed. It was high in the chest, on his right side, but he had bled a great deal.

"Got a fire in the kitchen stove?" Womack asked.

"Yes."

"Heat some irons. We've got to warm him up. Fetch some whisky and hot water if you've got it."

"The kettle's on the front of the stove. It'll be hot in a minute."

"Some clean cloth, too."

Nodding, she swung out of the room. When she returned, Womack had finished undressing Hovey. "Bullet went through him," he said. "Nice, clean hole. Trouble is, he got so awful damned cold."

He washed the wound and doused it with whisky, Rose standing beside him, the lamp in her hand. She asked tonelessly, "How did the bullet go in?"

"From the back."

"Who do you think did it?"

There was little bleeding now. Womack bandaged the wound with the cloth she had brought and tucked the covers in around Hovey, his mind on the question Rose had asked. He said finally, "I don't know," and let it go at that.

Rose put the lamp back on the bureau. "Is there anything we can do, Bill? Do we have to just stand here and wait for him to die?"

"We can keep him warm. That's all. If he was younger and stronger, he'd make out fine."

"And if he hadn't drunk so much." She turned toward the door. "I'll start supper."

"Fetch them irons in as soon as they're hot," he called.

Womack sat down beside the bed, feeling the warmth from the potbellied stove in the front room. He got up and walked around, rubbing his hands. He had been colder than he had realized.

Rose came in presently with three irons wrapped in paper. Womack placed them under the covers close to Hovey and felt his pulse. He said, "If he comes around, give him a shot of whisky."

"Where are you going?"

"Take care of my horse."

"Don't stay out there long." She stared at her father's face, slack and expressionless, its network of purple veins dark against his white skin. "I'm afraid, Bill. I'm terribly afraid."

"Nothing to do now but wait."

She raised her eyes to him. "We should have gone away. Dad wanted to last year, when Chapman made us an offer, but Ed and I talked him out of it. This is home to us."

"And you wouldn't run."

She nodded. "But it would have been better if we had."

"I don't think so. I've seen people who ran. Gets to be a habit, once you start."

Picking up the lantern, Womack left the house. The air was filled with snow, fat flakes that would pile up fast if they continued coming down like this. He was chilled again before he got back to the house. He took off his hat and slicker and stood beside the stove, his hands held over it. The house was filled with the smell of frying meat. It brought to Womack a consciousness of his hunger, and he waited impatiently until Rose called, "Supper's ready."

Womack stepped into Hovey's room and felt him. His body was warmer and his pulse much stronger. Womack tucked the covers back around him and listened a moment to his labored breathing. He'd get lung fever, lying out there as he had, and filled with more whisky than three men should have drunk. He'd live for only a day or two, Womack thought; and when he went into the kitchen and looked at Rose's taut, pale face, he knew he didn't have to tell her.

Womack drank two cups of steaming coffee before he began to eat. Rose said apologetically, "I bragged too soon about how good a cook I was. I—I got this on as soon as I could."

"Best chuck I ever et," he said around a mouthful of steak.

"What happened at Lowrie's?"

He told her, adding: "I didn't know what to do with a man who could lie like that. I could have pulled a gun on him, but I figured the sign wasn't right. I had a notion he'd stick to his lying regardless."

"I should have told you about him," she said. "He doesn't talk much, and when he does, nobody believes him. He did say one thing that was true, though. You'll never convince Chapman that Lowrie has enough courage to double-cross him."

"Got any more irons?"

She nodded. "They're on the stove. I thought I'd

take them to him as soon as we're done eating. Bill, don't you have any idea what happened?"

"How could I? I found him not more'n a hundred yards from the house. It's my guess he was shot a long ways from here and passed out where I found him."

"It must have been Chapman, but why? He knew Dad wouldn't fight him. He never has. He'd get mad and blow off to Ed and me, but when it came right down to it he'd get on his knees every time."

Womack nodded, saying nothing. He remembered how it had gone in the back room of the Starlight, but he was remembering, too, the talk he'd had with Hovey in the barn that morning. Courage, he knew, ran in queer streaks. It was possible that Grant Hovey had reached the end of his string and that he'd braced Chapman, who, realizing that Hovey in this mood might be dangerous, had shot him in the back after he'd left.

When they finished eating, Rose wrapped the irons that were on the stove, and Womack carried them into her father's room. He removed the cool irons and placed the hot ones beside him. There seemed to be no change in his condition except that his breathing was a little louder and more labored.

They returned to the kitchen, and Womack took off his money belt. He counted the money Ed had given him in Denver and laid it on the table, saying: "You hired me to keep your dad out of trouble, and I failed. I don't take money for a job I don't do."

"That's crazy talk," she cried. "You had no way of knowing he was going to ride out this morning and get himself shot. You keep that money."

"Can't do it," he said. "I've got my notions about things like this. I deliver the goods or I don't get paid. That's all there is to it."

She glared at him for a moment, angry and defiant, then her spirit seemed to go out of her. "If anyone is to blame, it's me and Ed for not selling out when Dad wanted to."

He picked up the coffeepot and filled his cup, asking, "What does Chapman think about you and Ed fetching in some good bulls?"

She walked to the table and sat down. Her lips were trembling, but she did not let herself cry. Womack took a chair across from her, feeling the intensity of her emotion. He rolled a smoke, thinking it would be good for her if she could talk.

"He told us not to get them," she said finally. "He claimed we're doing all right, and he didn't want the combine broken up. Paddy Ryan loaned us the money. It was the only time I know of when he didn't knuckle down to Chapman. I don't think Chapman knows it yet."

"You and Ed figured on pulling out of the combine and running your herd separate. That it?"

She nodded. "We've been ashamed of Dad for a long time. That's why we wouldn't let him sell. We told him to go ahead if he wanted to, but we were staying here on the mesa, so he turned Chapman down. We aimed to keep our cows here and put them on the high country east of us. We don't have to use the Angel Peak country."

"What about winter range?"

"We talked to Moran. He was going to let us winter along the river. It's lower, and the weather is never as bad as it is on the mesa. I don't think we'd have any winter loss, and we always do now."

"Chapman know you'd talked to Moran?"

She shook her head. "He doesn't even know why Ed went to Denver. When we talked about pulling out of the combine and buying bulls, he said No, and he thought that's all there was to it."

Womack drank his coffee and put the empty cup down. "Did this idea have anything to do with hiring me?"

She stared at her hands, which were folded on her lap. "It had everything. It just seemed that nothing would be right until Chapman was dead. I'm ashamed of it now. It seems so—so selfish and cowardly, using you to do something we couldn't do, or didn't have the courage to do." She looked up, suddenly defiant. "But we couldn't run, and we couldn't keep on bowing down like Dad's done as long as we could remember. We just didn't know what to do."

"Justice," Womack said softly. "Funny word."

"All right, say it," she cried. "You think I didn't mean what I said on the stage, but I do. Ed and I were selfish and afraid and proud. I'll admit that, but folks ought to have the right to do what they want to, and we don't."

"I didn't say you didn't mean it. I was thinking that justice is something every man sees a little different. Chapman's got his notions about it, I reckon. Like with his wife and Lowrie, maybe, if he knows."

"I—I never thought of that. I suppose he does."

Womack rolled another cigarette. "I was thinking we ought to shuffle and deal again."

She rose, sick with misery. "I know. You're giving back the money, and you'll say I don't owe you the thousand dollars Ed promised I'd pay. You'll take the stage out tomorrow, and—"

"Didn't aim to." He fired his cigarette. "I told you about that little spread in South Park. I've been thinking that maybe this is better cow country right here. If I'm out of line, say so, but it struck me that maybe you'd let me throw in with you and Ed. Kind of give me something to hold to." He shook his head. "I'm sick of everything I've done and been. From now on, I aim to fight for what's mine, and not because somebody gives me an order."

She dropped back into the chair. "You want to swap your gun for a half interest in the Bow and Arrow?"

He stared at her through the smoke, feeling small and mean. He said, "You must hate me."

"No, no. I just wanted to know."

"I've got a little more to offer than my gun," he said. "It's money that makes the mare go, and it's lack of money that'll lick you. You had to borrow from Ryan to buy bulls. I reckon it took all you had to hire me. That right?"

"That's right."

"Well, if Chapman ain't whittled down a few notches, Ryan won't go on backing you. What happens then?"

"We'll walk out," she said. "Broke."

"All right. I've got about $10,000. I'll throw it into the pot. We'll build a fence between your range and Chapman's. We'll buy some more bulls and we'll hire a few hands who ain't afraid to smell powder smoke. We'll give Chapman a run for his money. We'll lick him, Rose, and it won't be just some drifting gunslick who's fighting him."

She began to cry then, the tears that she had held back for so long running unashamedly down her cheeks. Womack rose and came around the table. He laid a hand on her shoulder, saying softly: "No reason for that. I'm just asking for a chance. That's all I want."

She shivered, her shoulders hunched, then she dug a handkerchief out of her pocket and wiped her eyes. "You don't understand, Bill. It's everything we ever dreamed of, Ed and me: money enough to fight Chapman and a partner who isn't afraid of him. We've been so ashamed because we've been afraid."

"Nothing to be ashamed of. Everybody's afraid some time or other. I'm scared, too."

She looked up, startled. "Not you."

He grinned. "Sure, but Chapman don't know it. That's the trick. Never let the fellow you're fighting know how you feel." He walked back to his chair, holding under a tight rein the urge to tell her that everything he wanted was here, holding back more than he told her, much more. This was not the time. He asked, "Is it a deal?"

"Oh, yes," she said. "Of course it is. No matter what happens to Dad, it's a deal."

"Ed?"

"I'll answer for him. We think alike, Bill. We always have. I guess twins are that way."

He reached for the makings, a peace within him that he had not felt for a long time. Here was something to hold to at last, something that was his to fight for; this was the final break with his old life. He glanced at her, wondering if she sensed what was really in his mind.

"I'll see Paddy Ryan and have him send to Cheyenne for my dinero," he said. "And I'll see Chapman. He ain't had any real trouble yet, and I aim to have a little fun telling him."

Chapter 12: Accusation

WOMACK CHANGED THE IRONS AGAIN AND REMAINED BE-side Hovey's bed while Rose did the dishes. When she finished, she came into the bedroom to stand beside him, asking, "Any change?"

"No."

"He'll die, won't he?" When Womack did not answer, she said, "I know. You don't have to spare my feelings." She paused, breathing hard, then added, "I wish I knew how it happened."

"He may come around and be able to tell us. You'd better go to bed. I'll sit up with him."

She shook her head. "I couldn't sleep. I—"

The front door opened and a man called, "Rose."

"It's Ed," the girl cried, and ran out of the bedroom.

Womack followed. Rose was in her brother's arms, and he was saying excitedly: "I got the bulls. They'll be in Colatas by the end of the week. You oughta see 'em, Rose. They're flat as a table across their backs. Alongside them, our critters ain't nothing but hoofs, horns, and a beller, but we'll—" He saw Womack and stopped, startled. "Howdy, Womack. Didn't know you were here."

"I'm glad you're back," Womack said.

Rose stepped away from Ed, glancing at Womack and biting her lower lip. Ed peeled out of his coat and shook the snow from it, then dropped it over a chair and laid his hat on it. He sensed that something was wrong, and asked, "What's up?"

"Dad's been shot." Rose motioned toward the bedroom. "He's in there, unconscious. He won't live, Ed. I know he won't."

Ed crossed the living room in long strides, Rose behind him. A moment later they came back, the boy's face showing the shock that the sight of his father had given him. He asked, "How did it happen?"

"I don't know," Womack said. "I found him beside the trail. He'd been plugged earlier in the day and quite a ways from here, I'd say. Looked like he'd been laying there a long time."

"Where was he hit?"

"In the chest. From the back. The wound's pretty high, but the trouble is, he laid out there too long."

Ed dropped into a chair, gaze turning to Rose, and at that moment he was a kid with a man's body, an adolescent boy who looked to his sister for help and strength. He asked tonelessly, "What are we going to do?"

"Nothing now," she told him. "We'll just have to sit up with him and see that he stays warm. Maybe he'll be able to tell us how it happened."

"Nobody had nothing against him," Ed said, his voice trembling. "He just—"

He couldn't bring himself to say it, but Womack knew what was in his mind. He had started to say that

Grant Hovey wasn't worth killing. Nobody, not even his own children, had any real respect for him, and Hovey had known that. Womack was sure that neither Ed nor Rose had any idea why their father had bowed to Chapman, and he hoped they never would.

"Only thing to do is wait," Womack said. "If he's able to talk, we'll know who to go after. There'll be time enough then."

"But he was shot in the back—" Rose began.

"I know," Womack cut in, "but he was gone most of the day. If we can find out where he went and what he did, we'll know." He hesitated, choosing his words carefully because he didn't want to hurt them, and he couldn't tell them what Hovey had said that morning. He went on, "There's one thing my business has learned me. Sometimes a man gets so tired of the way he's been living that he goes a little crazy. Does something you'd never think he would."

"What are you driving at?" Ed demanded.

"Rose told me what you two wanted to do and that Chapman said No. As long as Chapman figures he needs the combine, he'll do everything he can to keep you in line. Well, your dad knew that. Maybe he knew a lot of things you never gave him credit for. It's my guess he rode over to the CC today and braced Chapman."

"You're loco," Ed said bitterly. "He wouldn't do nothing of the kind. I've known him for more'n twenty years. He just didn't have the guts." He stared at Womack defiantly. "I know, I tell you. He'd crawl from here to hell and back if Chapman told him to."

"I don't know." Rose laid a hand on her brother's shoulders. "He loved us when he was sober enough to think about it. Maybe Dad just couldn't stand it any longer. I—I'd like to think it was that way."

Ed's hands fisted. "So would I, but I don't believe it, and I ain't gonna do no bawling if he cashes in. He was never nothing to be proud of. All the time I was coming home, I figured he'd give us hell for buying the bulls. He'd rear up and say Chapman wouldn't stand for it and we couldn't fight him."

"I think you're wrong," Womack said. "Maybe he was proud of you, but he knew what Chapman would do. Maybe he was trying to keep you out of trouble."

"Proud!" the boy cried. "Proud! Why, hell, he didn't know what the word meant."

"Hush up, Ed." Rose shook his arm. "You hush that up."

Ed got up and walked toward the stove. "I saw Ryan when I was in town. He told me about you going to Slade's. He said you had forty-eight hours to keep the pot from boiling over. It ain't long enough, Womack."

"It was the best deal I could get," Womack said. "There are a lot of angles here you didn't tell me about in Denver. Maybe you didn't know about 'em, but they're coming out. It's the way it works when a fellow like me sits in on the game. Sort of like putting a poultice on a boil. Brings it to a head."

"We don't owe Slade nothing," Ed said truculently. "Why don't you let 'em fight it out?"

"We don't owe Slade nothing," Womack admitted, "but when a thing like this blows up you never know who's going to get hurt. I couldn't keep your dad out of trouble, and that was what you hired me for, but I aim to keep you and Rose out of it." He grinned. "I promised Chapman I'd clear this range. I'll do it, come hell or high water, but I didn't tell him he was the one I aimed to clear. If he shot your dad, I'll get him."

"That's my chore," Ed shouted. "He's my dad."

"No, it's my chore," Womack said gently. "This is my game, and I know how to play it. Before this is over I may need your help, but until I ask for it you stay out."

"That's right," Rose said. "It's our reason for bringing him here."

Ed was silent. He stood with his back to the stove, a gangling kid in whom the seeds of manhood were sprouting. After a long moment he shrugged his shoulders, still scowling, as if unconvinced. He said: "All right, Womack. You call the turn."

Womack picked up his hat. "I reckon you two can get along. I oughta be in town."

"It's a hell of a night to ride," Ed objected.

"I know that. Wonder if I can borrow a coat."

"I'll get Dad's," Rose said, and went into the kitchen.

"Still snowing?" Womack asked.

Ed shook his head. "It's cold, though."

Rose returned with her father's sheepskin coat. It was too big for Womack, but it would do. He buttoned it and put on his hat, then picked up his slicker.

"I don't look for anything much to happen yet," Womack said, "but it's hard to outguess Chapman. Better keep the house locked and your guns handy."

"He's too smart to try anything like that," Ed said. "The sheriff wouldn't stand for it. He's one man who ain't afraid of Chapman."

"Maybe not, but he's with the crew, so Chapman ain't worried about him. Besides, Chapman can blame anything that happens on Slade." Womack picked up the lantern and lighted it. "Just be careful. When this thing does bust, it'll rip right down the middle."

Rose put a hand out toward him. "Be careful, Bill."

"Sure." He winked, ignoring the anxiety that was in her. "Anyhow, I reckon we know who lit that fuse you wanted me to find."

"Who?"

"Nita, which ain't no surprise to you, but it makes it mighty rough for me. I don't know how to fight a woman." Nodding, he went out.

Womack rode westward, the sky clear now, the stars glittering with cold, distant brilliance. He pulled the collar of his sheepskin up around his neck, but he was cold before he had gone a mile. The wind flowing down the mountain knifed into his bones. He did not know what the weather should be like in this country, but it seemed to him that winter had come too soon.

He thought about the cattle that were still in the high country. Bow and Arrow could not afford a big loss. Now that he was going to be a partner, it would be his loss as well as the Hoveys'. He reached the CC before it struck him that he had forgotten to say anything to Ed about buying in with them, but perhaps it was just as well. The boy was in no condition to think or talk intelligently about it. That could wait until later.

Chapman's big house was ablaze with lights when Womack turned in from the road. It had snowed very little there, and at the moment the wind had died down. He racked his mount in front of the house beside another horse and went up the path, wondering who was there. Garrity, perhaps, who had decided it was time to tell Chapman what he had guessed about Womack. It probably didn't make any difference, not if Grant Hovey had said his piece that morning. Womack yanked on the bell pull, hearing the clear metallic jangle deep inside the house. While he waited, he unbuttoned his coat and eased his gun in leather. He did not expect trouble, but if Garrity was there, anything could happen.

A fat Mexican woman opened the door and stared at him, shivering involuntarily as the cold air touched her. Womack asked, "Is Mr. Chapman here?"

"Si, señor, but he is busy—"

"He'll see me." Putting a shoulder to the door, Womack shoved it open and went in. He closed the door, grinning at the angry woman. "It's mighty cold out there. Ain't smart, trying to heat the whole out-of-doors like that."

"Who is it, María?"

Womack glanced up. Nita was standing at the top of an open stairway that rose from the far side of the room. There was a big lamp on the massive oak table in the center of the room, but the light did not reach all the way up the stairway, and from where Womack stood he could not see Nita's face clearly.

"Womack, Mrs. Chapman," he said. "I want to see your husband."

She came quickly down the stairs, saying softly: "It's all right, María. I'll talk to him."

But Señor Chapman, he say—"

"I told you I'd talk to him," Nita said sharply. "It's all right. Go on back into the kitchen."

The woman hesitated, uncertain of her duty, then turned and waddled in her heavy-footed way across the room. When the kitchen door closed, Nita, standing at the foot of the stairs, asked in a low tone, "What do you want, Womack?"

He crossed to her, noticing that she was wearing a riding skirt and leather jacket, and that a coat and scarf had been dropped on the couch beside the big fireplace. He had a hunch that something was about to happen and that he'd come at the wrong time, but it was a vague feeling which might be only the result of the tension of the moment.

"I want to see Chapman."

"You're not working for him," she said. "Why did you come here?"

He hesitated, wondering how she had heard. She was not like the Nita Chapman he had talked to in town. Then she had been coolly self-possessed and certain of herself. Now she was hesitant and afraid, as if she had committed herself to a certain course of action and was questioning whether it was the right thing to do.

"How do you know I'm not working for Chapman?" Womack asked.

She made a quick dismissal of the question with a motion of her right hand. "Listen, Womack. I don't have much time. You've kicked up hell since you came here. I asked you to get out of the country, and you wouldn't do it. Now I'll pay you if you'll leave. I'll pay you more than the Hoveys can."

"Garrity tell you I was working for the Hoveys?"

"He guessed it, and Grant Hovey told Cole the same thing this morning." She glanced at the hall that made a long passage through the middle of the house, and brought her eyes back to Womack. "I told you Cole would throw his partners overboard when it suited him. He's done that with Hovey already."

Womack nodded. "Yeah, I figured that was it. I picked him up on the trail."

"Dead?"

"Mighty near it. Who plugged him?"

"Todd Jarvis."

"You see it?"

"No, but it had to be him. He came down from the cow camp to see if Cole wanted the herd started down from the mountains. He was here when Hovey left. I was gone, but María told me. Cole and Hovey had a terrible quarrel, and Hovey said he'd kill Cole if he didn't let his kids go ahead with their own herd. Cole said he couldn't do that. He didn't want the combine broken up and he didn't want another outfit on this side of the mesa. Hovey left and Todd followed him. María said she heard a shot. You'll be next, Womack, if you don't get out of the country."

Chapter 13: Ultimatum

WOMACK STOOD MOTIONLESS, STARING AT THE WOMAN'S tortured face as he thought about what she had said. It sounded like the truth. He said finally: "I guess that'd be about what happened. I still want to see Chapman. Where is he?"

She gripped his arms frantically, and he saw that she was close to hysteria. "Listen to me, you fool. You have nothing to gain on this range except a bullet in the back if you stay. Why don't you take what I can give you and get out?"

"How much?"

"What do you want?"

He laughed softly. "More'n you got to give. Or is Cole backing your offer?"

"No, no. He doesn't know anything about it."

"Then where would you get any money?"

"None of your business, but I'll get it. How much do you want?"

"Now you listen. I ain't leaving because I've got something here that's more important to me than all the money in Dogdance. I'll play this game out to the finish, and before I'm done I'll whittle Cole Chapman down to size."

"Will you do it now?"

He stared at her, puzzled. "You change a little too fast for me. I don't savvy what you've got in your noggin."

"I can't tell you." She put a hand to her face, swaying a little, and for an instant he thought she was going to faint. Then she regained control of herself. "I mean, I just can't stand it here any more. I used to think that money was everything, but I've lived with Cole for three years. It was a mistake, a bigger mistake than you or anyone else will ever know, because you don't know what I've been through. I'm leaving tonight. Will you help me?"

He shook his head. "This is a family game. It ain't my style."

"I wonder," she whispered. "The Hovey twins brought you here. You aren't in love with the girl, are you?"

He hesitated, knowing he could not trust her, but still feeling that whatever scheme she had in mind was bound to affect all of them. He said, "Yes, that's it."

"We've got the same problem, then. Can't you see that? As long as Cole's alive and has the power he has

now, you won't have any more happiness than I
have—not if you want Rose Hovey; but if we work
together—"

"You and me can never work together," he said
roughly. "Now are you going to tell me where Chapman is?"

She hesitated, anger working in her, but before she
could answer, steps sounded in the hall. Womack
wheeled. Black Garrity stood there, as immaculate as
ever, the superficial smile on his lips.

"Well, it's the fabulous Womack," Garrity said.
"I've been wondering when you'd show up."

"I came here to see Chapman, but his wife don't
want to tell me where he is."

Garrity pinned his dark eyes on Nita. "Why didn't
you fetch him in?"

"I wanted to talk to him," she said sullenly.

"You talk too damned much. I told you that in
town, and I'm telling you again. If you had judgment
of men, you'd see that Womack is one hombre you'll
never use."

"I need help," she cried. "If you were any kind of a
brother—"

She stopped, frightened, a hand coming up to her
throat, eyes wavering from Womack to Garrity.
Womack thought: So that's it. They're brother and
sister, and nobody's supposed to know.

"You finally had to let it out," Garrity said with
biting malice. "Well, it doesn't make much difference
now. I've got a notion Womack won't live very long.
Maybe not long enough to tell anybody."

"No, it doesn't make much difference," Nita whispered. "I told you there wasn't any sense in keeping it
a secret."

"Chapman know?" Womack asked.

"Sure." Garrity shrugged. "We didn't tell it around
because it seemed better if folks didn't know that Cole
Chapman's wife was a sister to a saloon man and a
gambler: the old business of social classes that has

cursed the world from the beginning. Nita had to be respectable, you know."

"Yeah, I know," Womack said.

"You ought to. Funny thing, isn't it? You don't get away from it even out here in a stinking hole like this. Classes! The sheep and the goats! The sheep need the goats, but they hate like hell to admit it." He frowned, staring at Nita, as if suddenly wondering why she was wearing the riding skirt and leather jacket. "Are you up to something?"

"How could I be?" she demanded. "On a night like this?"

Garrity took a step toward her, irritation showing on his usually bland face. "I forgot you don't like cold weather." He scratched the back of his neck, indecision gripping him. "You're a smart woman, Nita, too smart to throw away a hand that's as good as you're holding. I hope to hell you won't forget it."

"I'd have a hard time forgetting it as often as you remind me of it."

Garrity stood there a moment, still undecided, then wheeled toward the hall, jerking his head at Womack. "Come on. Cole's in his office." Womack followed, wondering if Garrity had seen the woman's coat and scarf on the couch.

The door into Chapman's office was open. Garrity went in, saying, "Womack's here to see you, Cole."

Womack stopped in the doorway. Chapman was seated at a huge mahogany desk, a neat pile of papers in front of him. He peered at Womack through his thick glasses, frowning, as if he wondered what had brought Womack here. Then he said: "Good evening, Womack. Come in and sit down."

"Thanks. I'll stand."

Womack moved through the door to put his back to the wall, wondering if the CC ramrod, Todd Jarvis, had gone back to the cow camp. He glanced around the room, discovering another surprising side to this most surprising man.

Usually a rancher's office was crammed with battered furniture, including a spur-scarred desk, saddles and bits of leather, guns and tally books, all brought together carelessly in one room and adding up to the disorder that most cowmen seemed to favor. But there was no disorder here. There were a few chairs, a bookcase that stood against the far wall and was filled with books, a few pictures on the wall of Colorado mountain scenes, and a county map. The desk, polished to a fine sheen, revealed not a single scar. Even the floor was covered by an expensive maroon rug. This was Chapman's room, just as the hotel room was Nita's. It was Womack's guess that Chapman spent a great deal of time here.

The rancher leaned back in his chair, amused. "What do you think of it, Womack?"

"Quite an office," Womack said.

"I don't suppose you ever saw one like it." Chapman pulled a drawer open and took a cigar from it. "You never saw a man like me, neither." He closed the drawer, asking with cool insolence, "Want a cigar, Womack?"

"No, thanks."

Womack reached for the makings, feeling Garrity's probing eyes on him. They were playing this out, wondering what he wanted and how much he knew. He had no doubt that Chapman had a gun on his lap. The first quick move on Womack's part would bring both Chapman's and Garrity's guns into action, and again he wondered if Todd Jarvis was around.

"Been out to Slade's?" Chapman asked.

"You know I was. Garrity told you."

Chapman shrugged. "So he did. I forgot. What did you find out?"

"Several things, but mostly I've got a question. The west end of the mesa don't have enough grass to be worth fighting over. Why are you trying to run Slade and his neighbors out of the country?"

"I don't like ten-cow ranches," Chapman said.

"They always steal from big outfits, and I don't propose to put up with it."

"That ain't good enough," Womack said. "Slade don't look like a cow thief to me."

Chapman eyed him for a moment. Then he said: "There are some other reasons. I'm the one who brought law and order to this country. The town belongs to me, figuratively speaking, as Garrity here says. Them that do the right things prosper. Them that don't fail. It's a simple matter of give-and-take, Womack. I give to those who take orders and I take from those that don't. Slade is one who don't take orders. I told you that."

"You're getting closer, now," Womack said. "You've got a notion you're big, and you're gonna cram that notion down everybody's throat. That it?"

Anger scorched Chapman's cheeks. He half rose, glancing at Garrity, then brought his gaze to Womack's face. He dropped back into his chair. He said: "You're right, friend. I am big, and I will cram that notion down people's throats, but that ain't all the answer yet. Take a look at the map."

Womack glanced at the map and shook his head. "I ain't much of a map reader. You'll have to tell me."

"All right, I will tell you. From Slade's place you couldn't see it, but farther west, between it and the Utah line, there's the prettiest valley in Colorado. It has the lowest altitude in the county, high walls that protect it from storms, and creeks that come down from the La Sals and flow the year around. We have considerable winter loss here on the mesa. If I had that valley to winter my she-stuff in, I'd have mighty near 100 per cent calf crop."

"And after you run Slade out, you keep on moving west and grab this valley."

"That's it in a nutshell." Chapman fingered the ash from his cigar. "It'll mean a little trouble. That's your meat. After we finish with Slade and his bunch, you'll have more work, your kind of work, Womack. Good pay. The law won't bother you. Why, hell, it's the sort of deal gun fighters dream about."

"Not me," Womack said.

Chapman grinned thinly, glancing at Garrity. "I thought so. You never fooled me, Womack. Not for a minute. I had a hunch about you before Black told me what he'd guessed and before Grant Hovey rode over this morning. I've got a hunch the Hovey girl is the answer to everything that's wrong with you. Funny thing what a man will do for a woman."

"You should know about that," Womack said.

Chapman took the cigar out of his mouth. He held it tilted in front of him, lips tightening into a bitter line. But he was not angry when he said: "Yes, I should know. I told you that the other day, too. I guess everybody knows but Nita."

"She knows, all right," Garrity said quickly. "She'll understand if you give her more time."

"Time." Chapman stared at his cigar. "There isn't enough time, Black. If I live to be a hundred years old, it wouldn't be enough time to prove to Nita that I'd give her anything she wants."

"Yes, there is," Garrity said. "It just takes patience."

Chapman put the cigar back into his mouth and pulled on it, the mood passing. "Well, Womack, now that you've turned the job down, I guess you'll be sloping out tomorrow."

"No," Womack said. "That's why I stopped here. I'm buying into the Bow and Arrow. Ed got back from Denver tonight. He bought some white-faced bulls. We're pulling out of the combine, Chapman."

He had expected this news to shock Chapman, but the CC owner showed no surprise. "I won't permit that. Drop your gun belt, Womack. Todd wouldn't mind blowing your head off with that scattergun. I think he'd kind of like to do it."

Womack made a slow turn toward the door, right hand hovering over gun butt. A big man stood there, a double-barreled shotgun in his hands. That would be Todd Jarvis. One look at his expressionless moon-round face told Womack he would do exactly as Chapman had said. There was nothing for him to do but drop his gun belt and step back from it.

Chapter 14: Under Garrity's Gun

CHAPMAN ROSE AND LAID HIS GUN ON THE DESK. "THAT'S fine. Take him along, Todd."

"This what happened to Hovey?" Womack asked.

"Something like that. I can't understand what got into the fool. Rode over here this morning boiling up like a coffeepot on a hot stove. Stayed a good part of the day, and I couldn't talk any sense into him. You can see how it would be, Womack. I couldn't afford to let him go around blowing off about a few of the things we've had to do. His kids will be easier to handle now, too, I think."

"Move," Jarvis said.

Womack hesitated, knowing he would not ride far. He died if he argued, he died if he obeyed.

Chapman, his face ugly now, motioned impatiently toward the door. "Get along. Your big name ain't no help to you now."

Womack turned toward the door as Jarvis backed into the hall. Womack remembered what Paddy Ryan had said, that Chapman had grown big with his help and the help of Garrity and Jarvis and Red Manion. Therein lay Chapman's real strength, securing obedience from men like that. Of the four of them, only

Ryan was rebellious. Jarvis was like a big dog, slow of mind but loyal and unquestioning.

A faint sound came to Womack then, of the front door opening and closing, and because he had no other weapon to use, he said slowly, "I think you just lost your wife, Chapman," and watched the brutal impact of his words on the man's round face, saw the muscle in his cheek begin to throb.

There was silence for a moment, a chill silence while Cole Chapman stood as motionless as if he were frozen. Then Garrity cursed; the words jumped out of him: "She was up to something. Damn her, I should have guessed."

Still Chapman did not move. Womack thought, He won't believe it because he don't want to believe it. He said, in the same slow, brutal way: "You owe me more'n you know, Chapman. She wanted help from me, and I wouldn't give it to her. Now she'll get it from Lowrie. She saw him today, and a real loving meeting it was."

"Where?" Chapman screamed. "Where?"

"South Cedar Creek canyon. This morning, before the storm."

"She was gone most of the day," Chapman whispered. "She came in this afternoon soaking wet."

They heard it then, all of them, the drum of a galloping horse on the frozen ground, and Chapman grabbed his gun and shoved it into leather.

"We'll get her, Todd," Chapman shouted wildly. "She'll be sorry until the day she dies." He limped out of the office in as much of a run as he could manage, calling back: "Keep Womack here. We'll take care of him when we get back."

Jarvis followed Chapman down the hall and into the front room. Garrity, who had drawn his gun, motioned toward Womack, his face anything but expressionless now. It was the face of a gambler who had staked everything on one deal and lost.

"Sit down, Womack," Garrity said. "If you ever see Nita again, you can thank her for giving you a few more hours of life, if that's worth thanking her for."

Womack didn't sit down. He heard the front door slam shut as Chapman and Jarvis went out, heard Chapman shout: "She took Garrity's horse, damn her to hell. She's headed for Lowrie's place. Get a move on, Todd. Saddle up."

Garrity had his head cocked, listening, eyes still on Womack. The gun belt that Womack had dropped was behind him. He thought of making a try for it, but gave up the idea at once. Nita had given him a few minutes, perhaps a few hours, that might bring him a better chance than this, if he had any luck.

Womack stood motionless, watching Garrity's bleak face. Presently they heard Chapman and Jarvis ride away, headed south. Womack said: "Funny, Chapman going after a wife who don't want anything so much as to get away from him. What'll happen when he gets her back?"

"She'll be here," Garrity said.

"And what'll he have?"

"He can look at her. That's about all he's ever done since their wedding night."

"Don't seem like enough reason to drag her back here," Womack said.

"You'd have to know Cole to understand. I guess it doesn't make much sense, but Cole's what he is. You can't judge him like you would any other man."

Casually Womack moved around the desk and sat down on it. He said: "If they go to Lowrie's place, they'll be gone a long time. Let's hear the story about Nita. It's my guess she's what ails this range."

Womack was within five feet of Garrity. The gambler studied him for a time, dark eyes inscrutable. Then he said, quite casually: "You jump me and I'll kill you. You know that, don't you?"

Womack shrugged. "When they get back, Jarvis will

do the job, so what the hell. Chapman's made up his mind."

"He don't aim to let you throw in with the Hovey twins. That's why."

"Forgot all about Slade, looks like."

"No. He'll take care of that chore after the boys fetch the herd down. That's the trouble with a deal like this. Cole can't turn back once he starts something."

"What about Nita?"

Garrity scooted his chair back against the wall, and taking a cigar from his pocket, began to chew on it. "Doesn't make much difference whether you know the story or not. Might help pass the time. Well, Nita and me had an Irish father and a Spanish mother. Made quite a combination. Nita got the fire and the beauty, and I got the brains. Neither one of us has much of a conscience, whatever that is.

"She's a lot younger than I am. After our folks died, I tried to take care of her. Had her in a convent when she was a kid. Then put her in a school in Santa Fe. I knew I'd never be anything else but what I am, and I wanted Nita to have a different life; but all I've done is to make a mess out of everything."

Garrity chewed on his cigar for a time, silent. Womack, watching him, sensed that the man was tortured by a hell that was of his own making, and that now he saw no escape from it.

"She ran away from school after I came here," Garrity went on. "I found her in Silver City. We had quite a row, but she made it clear that culture and respectability were two things she didn't want. Well, I fetched her here, although we made it look like she'd just drifted in. She fixed up those hotel rooms, and right off Cole got interested, like I figured he would; but I didn't figure on Abner Lowrie wanting her. To make it worse, she fell in love with him, and that's the last thing I ever dreamed of."

"Judging from what I saw today," Womack said, "she still is."

Garrity nodded. "She never got over it. That was my mistake. I talked her into marrying Cole. The notion of living with Lowrie on that rundown ranch of his didn't appeal to her, and Cole made a lot of promises. The trouble was, Cole is a man who shouldn't ever have got married, least of all to a woman like Nita, who expects something out of a man. It's been pretty bad since then, and the worse it got, the more Cole wanted to keep her."

"He knows about Lowrie?"

"He doesn't know how bad it is. Or I'll put it this way: Lowrie's a liar and double-crosser. Cole knows that, but where he missed was thinking the fellow is a coward. Cole thought Lowrie would take orders and let Nita alone because he was afraid to do anything else, and I couldn't convince him that Lowrie's been in cahoots with Slade all the time. We all know Lowrie killed his dad, and he aims to get Cole when he sees a good chance. It's my guess he's the one who shot at you the other night."

"Then he's a coward," Womack said angrily. "Nobody but a coward would dry-gulch a man."

"I'd say he's just careful. He thought Slade would beef you, but on the chance you'd get away, he was watching for you here in town. He didn't want you telling around he'd been out there at Slade's, and he didn't want you to get Slade and his bunch sidetracked. I'm guessing now, but it strikes me he's counting on a range war to beef Cole so it wouldn't look bad for him."

"Another dry-gulching job would raise hell after what happened to his dad. That it?"

"That's it. It'd be different with you. Most folks hereabouts would be happy to see you dead, and nobody's going to ask too many questions abou it if you get plugged. But he's got to be careful with Cole because he wants to marry Nita." Garrity chewed on his cigar for a time. "You see, Lowrie lost about everything he had in a poker game with Cole. Marrying Nita would be one way to get it back, but I can't make Nita see that the ornery son is after the CC and isn't really in love with her."

"But that ain't the point with Nita," Womack said. "She wants to get away from Chapman."

"I know, but she's in love with Lowrie," Garrity said. "Getting away from Cole isn't all of it. I'm thinking about her, and I know Lowrie will never care about her happiness."

Womack leaned forward. "Then you're gonna have to decide between her and Chapman. Don't look like you'd want her to stay here, living with Chapman and hating him like she does."

"I've had some big plans," Garrity said tonelessly, "for Nita and me both. Cole trusts me. I've done him a few good turns. Long as he's top dog, I've got a good thing. If he loses out, I'll lose out. We're tied up pretty close, me and Manion and Jarvis and Cole. In the end Nita would be better off if she stuck with us."

"What about Ryan?"

"He's an old man. He doesn't count much either way."

"He loaned Rose and Ed the dinero to buy the bulls with."

"And he'll be damned sorry when he sees they're licked."

"I don't think Nita will go to Lowrie's place," Womack said. "She's smart enough to know Chapman would look for her there."

Garrity nodded. "She may go to town. Well, it won't make any difference. Cole's bound to find her, and she'll wind up back here."

"You think you can forget she's your sister?"

Garrity canted his chair back against the wall and gave Womack a long stare. He said finally: "You're pretty smart, but what you don't see is that there's some things I can't do. Going back on a man who is my friend is one of them."

"Suppose she gets out of the country? Maybe she'll take the train at Colatas and go to Denver."

"She won't. She hasn't got much money, and she's in love with Lowrie." Garrity's gun lay across his lap, his hands fisted on his knees. "That's where I've missed on the whole thing. I thought that being married to Cole, even if it wasn't a real marriage, would be enough to satisfy her. Cole's given her all the comforts and luxuries a woman could want, but it hasn't been enough. I've known some women to do crazy things because they were in love, but I didn't think Nita would act like she has about Lowrie."

"She jumped the gun tonight, didn't she?"

"She jumped the gun all right," Garrity said grimly. "I told her she was crazy, but she thought she could get you to leave. Then Lowrie could play out his hand like he planned, and there'd be a showdown between Slade's bunch and the combine. But I guess she just couldn't stand it any longer." Garrity jerked the cigar out of his mouth and threw it across the room. "You're a fool, too, Womack. You won't get anywhere playing with the Hovey twins. What's got into you?"

"What's sucking around after Chapman got you?"

"Business," Garrity answered. "Security. The law's on my side. I don't need to worry about whether this is going to be the last day I'll live, and I'm guessing it's been a long time since you could say that. I know your kind. You'll never change. You can't. You've made your name and you can't get away from it. You'll wind up with some trigger-happy kid's slug in your back."

"It'll change," Womack said. "I won't keep on living the way I have." He took a step toward Garrity, his fists clenched, irritation in him because he knew the gambler was right.

Garrity gave him a thin smile and shook his head.

"Funny thing. When a man like you goes soft, he gets just as soft as he was tough; and that makes him easy for somebody to plug, somebody he never figured would try it."

"Tell me something," Womack said softly. "How are you going to feel when Chapman fetches Nita back? I mean, down inside your soul—if you've got one. You'll be thinking about how you fixed this in the first place, and you'll look at Nita and see all the misery that's in her. How'll you feel then?"

"I told you there were some things I can't do," Garrity cried. "Nita's thrown away what I've tried to—"

Womack was standing within a single step of the gambler; the gun was still on the man's lap. There would be no better chance. He didn't wait for Garrity to finish what he had to say, but dived at him, giving him no warning of his intentions.

Garrity got the gun into his hands and threw a shot that burned like the passage of a red-hot iron along Womack's ribs, then Womack hit him on the side of the head. The chair slid out from under Garrity, and he hit the floor hard, but managed to retain his hold on the gun. He fired again, but the shot was wild. His fall had shaken him, and it took a moment to tilt his .44 upward at Womack. That small interval of time was long enough for Womack to pick up the chair and swing it downward. He knocked the gun out of Garrity's hand, the thunder of the gambler's second shot still hammering against the walls of the room.

Garrity fell flat, dazed by the blow. Scooping the gun up as Garrity struggled to his knees, Womack brought the barrel down in a brutal blow across the top of the other's head. Garrity was knocked cold. Womack laid the gun on the desk, not sure whether he had killed the gambler or not. Picking up his own gun belt, he buckled it around him and stepped into the hall.

The Mexican woman was coming, attracted by the shots. Womack met her in the living room. He said: "Get on back into the kitchen, Maria. Garrity's taking a nap."

She looked at his face, and without a word, turned and walked away. He waited until the kitchen door was closed, then ran out of the house and across the yard to the hitch rack. His horse was still there. Chapman had been too intent on his pursuit of Nita to consider the possibility that Womack might escape.

Mounting, Womack turned the horse toward town. There was no wind now, and the starshine made a faint silver glow on the thin fall of snow. It was then that the truth came to Womack: *Garrity had purposely given him this chance.*

Like many gamblers he had known, Black Garrity had his own unalterable code of loyalty. He would not turn on Cole Chapman, but he had seen in Womack a man who could free his sister. It was strange, perhaps unreasonable, but Womack was convinced it had been that way.

With that certainty, a new respect for Garrity was born in Bill Womack. Still, Garrity had not really settled anything by letting Womack escape. If Lowrie remained in the country, he would be killed; if Chapman was killed and Lowrie and Nita ran away and were married it would still be no different. Either way, Nita Chapman would not be happy.

Chapter 15: In Dogdance

WEARINESS HAD AT LAST CAUGHT UP WITH BILL WOMACK. He slept late, much later than he had intended, and woke with the thought that by six o'clock tonight the time he had bought from Ira Slade would be gone. He was doubtful if the man would make another deal. The little ranchers were desperate; they had lived with danger too long to be reasonable. Winter was at hand, they had no credit in town, and they had no market for the few steers they had to sell. Anything could happen now. The fuse that Rose had talked about was burning very close to the powder keg.

Womack had breakfast at the Chinaman's, then stepped into the barbershop next door and bought a shave. The barber maintained a stony silence until he was finished and Womack had paid him. Then he said, with sullen bitterness, "I should have let my hand slip just now."

"Why?"

"I was in the hotel lobby the other night with Kelsey and the rest of 'em after somebody took a shot at you."

Womack slipped into his sheepskin. "Well?"

The barber licked dry lips. "I've got a wife and four kids. All I want is to be let alone. Just a chance to work and raise them kids."

"I ain't taking that chance away from you."

"The hell you ain't. Who gets hurt when there's a big fight? Little fry like us, that's who, and I don't want my kids shot when the bullets start flying."

"Get 'em out of town."

"No place to take 'em."

"You didn't have to come here. It's a big country."

"But I am here. I've got my business. We own a home. You think it's right to get the short end of the stick because some drifting gun slinger comes and stirs up hell?"

Womack stared at the man's bitter, accusing face. He wondered what Rose would say to this. There was no justice in the barber's blaming him. He was handy; that was all. The seeds of this trouble had been sowed a long time ago. It was up to the barber and Joe Kelsey and the rest of the townsmen to defend themselves. But they wouldn't, or couldn't. They were all like the barber, these little men who wanted to be let alone; they would suffer if Dogdance became a battleground.

"Maybe there won't be any trouble," Womack said. "If there is, see that your wife and kids stay home."

He went out, Garrity's words plowing through his mind, "You've made your name and you can't get away from it." For a time he stood on the boardwalk, staring along the street that was strangely empty at a time of day when there should be some activity.

The sky had cleared and there was no wind, but the sun gave little warmth. The snow had not reached this far across the mesa, but to the south he could see Angel Peak. The snowfall had been heavy there, and he could make out the pattern of the winged figure that had given the mountain its name.

He thought of the night in Denver when Ed Hovey had knocked on his hotel door. These last few days had been an illusion; he was facing reality again. He should have changed his name and followed his nose. He had been a fool to think he could escape his past; he had been a fool to let Rose get hold of his heart, to let his dreams fashion themselves around her. If Garrity or Todd Jarvis had killed him last night, she would have blamed herself; a sense of guilt would have left a scar upon her soul that would be there forever. And it would be the same if he died today or tomorrow. If he stayed on Dillon Mesa and bought into the Bow and Arrow as he planned, he would still be Bill Womack. As Garrity had said, he'd wind up with a bullet in his back from some trigger-happy kid. A hell of a world, he thought in a flash of bitterness, a damned sorry life when a man's past bound him so there was no escape. Here were the things he wanted: a woman, a home, respectability; and he could not even reach for them.

Womack glanced up at the pale sun. About noon. Six hours until the west-end bunch rode in. There was no telling what they would do. If Chapman hit town while they were here, it would break wide open. Now, with Nita gone, Chapman would be out of his head.

"A damned sorry life!" He said it aloud, his mouth thin and grim across his tanned face. He thought about Nita, feeling sympathy for her. He could even feel sympathy for Black Garrity. He glanced at the Starlight, wondering whether the gambler was back, what he would do if he was, and whether Nita was in her hotel room. All of them were caught up in a snarl of love and hate and inordinate pride and prodding ambition: Nita, who possessed more than her share of fire and beauty; Lowrie, who hated Chapman because the CC owner had assumed the position on Dillon Mesa that old Jake Lowrie had once held; and he, Womack, the self-appointed administrator of justice, he too was caught. He had his code just as Black Garrity had, a code that would not let him leave until everything was settled one way or another.

Womack walked to the bank, knowing that if anyone held the key to peace, it was Paddy Ryan; but he could not be sure the old man would use it.

Ryan was in the teller's cage waiting on a customer when Womack came in. He glanced up, saw who it was, and nodded. "Howdy, Womack. I'll be done here in a minute."

"No hurry," Womack said, and moving around the counter, sat down and rolled a smoke.

A moment later Ryan came up to him. "What's up?"

"Trouble."

Ryan glanced at his watch. "Noon. No wonder I was hungry. Let's go over to the hotel and put the feed bag on."

"Just had breakfast."

"Well, then, we'll hike over to the Starlight and have a drink. I always lock up at noon."

Womack shook his head. "I came in here to swap talk. Go lock up if you want to."

Ryan dropped into his swivel chair. "No need to, I reckon. Get on with the talking. I've been worried about you, boy."

"Been a little worried myself. You said the other day out at Slade's you wasn't a brave man. I aim to see."

"I ain't. I'll tell you that again."

Womack rubbed out his cigarette. "I don't believe you. It took some guts to loan the Hovey twins that dinero to buy their bulls. Garrity figures you'll back down when Chapman starts shoving."

Ryan leaned back in his chair, bony hands folded in front of him, his face impassive. "Garrity's wrong. I used to be a good gambler because I always played the percentages. Garrity plays the same way. That's why he said what he did, but there's a difference."

"You're still a good gambler, ain't you?"

"Not very. I'm an old man. When you get to my place in life, you'll find yourself thinking about what kind of defense you're gonna make when you face St. Peter. Loaning that dinero to Ed Hovey is one thing I've got on my side of the ledger."

Womack, studying the old banker's craggy face, decided that Rose was right about him. As long as there was a chance to win, Paddy Ryan would fight.

"Chapman's crazy," Womack said. "That makes him hard to figure. Once he starts this thing, he won't back down till he's dead, and he'll make it damned tough on anybody who's against him. It's like going through a door and locking it behind you."

Womack told him what had happened. Ryan listened, his face growing grave. When Womack finished, the banker said: "I ain't surprised about Nita, but I sure missed on Grant Hovey. It just goes to prove that you can't always tell what's a good bet and what ain't."

"The point right now is to keep Slade and his friends in line. Give Chapman enough time and he'll put a rope on his own neck, but Slade's bunch will be hard to handle unless you stop 'em."

"Me? Hell, I can't do anything. Jim Kelsey lit a shuck for his farm a while ago, and Red Manion is ten miles from here. We don't have any kind of a star toter in town."

"You can stop 'em," Womack said slowly, "if you're willing to loan 'em enough to get through the winter on. The trouble is, we may lose. If we do, Chapman will skin you and nail your hide on your front door."

Ryan rose and walked to a window. He stood there with his back to Womack, a gaunt old man. Without turning, he said in a low voice, "I savvy what you mean about locking the door." He stiffened and then wheeled toward the door. "Something's happened."

Womack got up and followed. Half a dozen townsmen burst in from the street, the barber in front, as panicky a lot as Womack had ever seen.

"They're coming," the barber yelled. "Slade and his whole bunch. A hundred of 'em. I told you—"

"All right," Womack said testily. "I'll handle 'em. Just see you don't start nothing."

They hesitated, eyeing Womack until Ryan said: "Go on. Git. You heard what he said."

"You've both been hanging with Chapman," the barber cried, "and Chapman wants them fellows off the mesa. You'll start throwing lead, and Slade will take it out on us."

"Damn it," Womack shouted. "Get out of here and stay off the street. There won't be no trouble if you don't start it."

They turned and ran. Womack gave Ryan a thin grin. "You'd have to look a long time to find a spoonful of guts in that whole bunch."

"You can't really blame 'em," Ryan said. "They've got families. It makes a difference."

Womack stepped into the street and waited in front of the bank. When Ryan joined him, he said: "Stay inside. I'll fetch Slade in when he gets here."

There was far from a hundred in the cavalcade that rode into town. Womack counted them: twelve. Some were men he had seen at Slade's place. The others were strangers, four of them boys, probably sons of Slade's neighbors, kids who had no business there.

Slade rode in front, a tired and bitter man who pinned smoldering eyes on Womack. They were dangerous, all of them; they were of a mind to force a showdown because they could no longer bear to wait; they had reached the point where they didn't care.

"You're ahead of time," Womack called, and stepped into the street.

Slade raised a hand and reined his horse to a stop. The others spread out around him, hands on gun butts, and Womack knew from the set of their faces that it would take very little to fan what was now a small glow of fire into a hungry, predatory flame.

"We aim to have a few drinks," Slade said in a truculent voice. "We'll wait till six like we agreed."

"What are your plans then?"

"If Chapman's around, we'll burn him down. If he ain't, we'll take this town apart at the seams. We'll bust Ryan's bank open and we'll help ourselves to the dinero he wouldn't loan us. We'll take the grub we need from the stores and then we'll go get our families. After that we'll just keep on riding."

"The owlhoot's a tough trail to ride, friend," Womack said.

"I reckon you'd know," Slade flung at him.

"I never rode it," Womack said, "but I've seen some good men who did. Men like you. You'll drag your women and kids through hell, and for what?"

"It's that or starve," Slade shouted. "It's that or wait till Chapman sends a gang to smoke us down. We've been dragging our wives and kids through hell, just sitting out there waiting. Can't be much worse."

Womack understood. He doubted that he could stop them without trouble; and if it came to that, he would be fighting for Chapman, the last thing he wanted to do.

"Come into the bank with me, Slade," Womack said. "We'll make a deal with Ryan."

The rancher shook his head. "No use, Womack. This is Chapman's town, and everybody here belongs to him. No reason we should trust you or anybody else."

"This is Chapman's town because the people are afraid of him and they ain't proud of it, but the biggest mistake you're making is the same one you made at your place. I ain't Chapman's man. He'll kill me if he gets a chance. He tried to last night."

A man next to Slade laughed. "Hogwash, Ira. Ever hear anything like it?"

"Never did," Slade answered. "Chapman's made talk about sending for a killer like you, Womack. Then you show up and say you ain't the one. I claim you're a liar, Womack. Don't take us for complete fools."

Doubt deepened in Womack, but he tried again, his eyes sweeping the half-circle of riders and coming again to Slade. He asked, "Where's Lud Pierson?"

Slade swore in a bitter voice. "He's with his sister Molly. Didn't have the guts to ride into town when it came right down to cases."

"Thought he was gonna get me."

"I said he didn't have the guts."

"I told you the other day that if you worked Pierson

over you'd find out something about Lowrie. You think he's your friend, and that's another mistake."

"And I'm still saying you're a liar," Slade shouted. "Get back on the walk, damn it. We're going to wait in the Belle Union."

Womack put his hand on gun butt. He said: "Slade, I don't want trouble. Send your men on down to the Belle Union, and you come in and talk to Ryan. I'm going after Pierson and I'll fetch him in. Before I'm done, he'll tell you the truth, and you'll find out a few things about Lowrie."

There was a moment of sullen silence, their stormy faces altered by curiosity. Then the man beside Slade said, "Why not, Ira?"

Slade nodded and reined toward the hitch pole in front of the bank. He said: "Go ahead, boys. I'll see what they've got to say."

Slade dismounted and tied as the rest rode on down the street, Womack stepping up on the walk. Slade joined him, eyeing him suspiciously. He asked, "If you ain't Chapman's hired man, just what in hell are you doing here?"

"The Hovey twins hired me to come here to keep their dad out of trouble. I wasn't able to do that. Todd Jarvis shot him in the back, and I reckon Hovey'll die, but maybe I can keep Rose and Ed out of trouble."

"So," Slade breathed, "Chapman's combine is breaking up."

Womack nodded. "Chapman's wife ran away from home. It's my guess she's with Lowrie."

A grin touched Slade's bleak face. "Now what do you know about that." The grin faded. "I still don't savvy why you want to save this miserable thieving burg. I know damned well you don't love it or us enough to want to keep us out of trouble."

"I'm thinking about myself," Womack said. "I'm buying in with the Hovey twins and I aim to stay here. Chapman's the one we've got to lick, and we can't do it fighting each other."

Slade frowned as he thought this over, and for the first time it seemed to Womack that the man was trying to believe him. Without another word he wheeled and walked into the bank. He said: "Womack claims you'll make a deal. Speak your piece, Ryan."

The banker stood in the teller's cage. He said hoarsely: "That's right, Ira. Come here." He pushed a piece of paper under the wicket.

Still suspicious, Slade moved to the teller's window. He picked up the paper, read it, and put it down, startled. "Everybody's loco today. This here's a note for $500."

"So it is," Ryan said dryly. "Sign it."

The banker dropped a handful of gold coins in front of Slade. The rancher cuffed back his dirty Stetson, asking, "What's the catch?"

"Let's say I'm trying to keep my bank from being robbed. You'd believe that, wouldn't you?"

"Won't work. We're fixing to help ourselves—"

"No, Ira," Ryan said. "You ain't an outlaw. Don't try making yourself one. Go get the rest of your bunch. I'll loan every rancher on the west end who owns his outfit the same amount I'm loaning you. It's enough to get through the winter. I told you the other day things would change."

"Figure that'll save your bank?"

Womack came up to stand beside Slade. "Listen, you chowder-headed idiot. Ryan's trying to do something decent, just like when he loaned the Hovey twins the money to buy some good bulls. When Chapman hears that Ryan jumped the track, he'll kill him if we don't get Chapman first. He's taking the risk, not you."

Slade scratched his stubble-covered chin, looking at Womack and then at Ryan. He asked again, "What's the catch?"

"There's just one," Womack said. "I told you I was going after Pierson. If Chapman rides in before I get back, there'll be hell to pay. The catch is, you're to keep your boys from getting drunk, but stay in town so Ryan will be safe."

"That's one thing I can do," Slade said, and picking up the pen Ryan offered him, scribbled his name.

Ryan was tugging at his beard, worried eyes on Womack. "That's a fool notion you got, boy. Pierson might be with his sister Molly, but she ain't worth a damn. Or he might be in Owl's Hole. If you go in there, you'll get plugged sure."

"I aim to try."

"You don't even know where the Hole is. I can't tell you, neither. You know where it is, Ira?"

"No," Slade said quickly. "It's across the river. That's all I know."

"I'll find out," Womack said, and turned toward the door.

"Wait a minute," Ryan called. "Just what good will it do if you fetch Pierson back?"

Womack swung around. "Plenty. Slade's got his twine tangled, trusting Lowrie like he is. If we're ever going to get the kinks out, this is the time. I want him for a neighbor, not an enemy."

"A neighbor," Ryan shouted. "Now what kind of talk—"

"I'm buying into the Bow and Arrow," Womack cut in.

"So that's it." Ryan turned to Slade. "Would you believe it if Lud told you Womack had to shoot Jim or get plugged himself?"

"I might," Slade said. "There's something wrong with Lud, or he'd have come with us today."

"Well, then," Ryan shouted, "why in thunder don't you go get Moran? Or Rose Hovey? Or the stage driver? They saw it, too."

"You can talk to Butch when he gets in," Womack said, "but it might be hard getting Moran up here, and I don't want to fret Rose about it. I've got another reason for fetching Pierson. Lowrie was the one who hired him and his brother to stick around Moran's station. I aim to make Pierson tell Slade what Lowrie's up to."

Ryan spread his hands. "All right. Go get yourself shot. You're the most mule-headed son I ever ran into."

"I've been told that before," Womack said dryly, and walked out.

Chapter 16: Molly Pierson

WOMACK WENT TO THE HOTEL BEFORE HE LEFT TOWN. HE asked the clerk, "Mrs. Chapman been in today? Or last night?"

The clerk shook his head. "Ain't seen her."

Womack turned and climbed the stairs. If Nita had come to her room, she was probably hiding, because she would not want her husband to know she was here. It was possible for her to have slipped in through the back some time during the night.

There was no answer when Womack knocked on her door. He hesitated, listening, but heard nothing that would indicate a woman's presence. He tried the door. It was unlocked. He turned the knob and shoved the door open, calling, "Nita." Still no answer. He stepped inside. The living room appeared to be unchanged. Slowly Womack moved to the bedroom, calling again, "Nita." Hollow echoes from a deserted room came back to him. He glanced into the bedroom. It was empty, and there was no indication that she had been there and hastily gathered her clothes.

For a moment Womack stood there, the certainty in him growing that Nita had not come to town after she

had left the CC. It was unlikely she had gone to the
Slash Triangle. If she had not left the country—and
Garrity had been sure she wouldn't—she must have
met Lowrie somewhere last night. They were probably
hiding out, perhaps in some line cabin or prospector's
shack.

Womack left the hotel and hired a horse in the
livery stable, a chestnut gelding that was not built for
speed but would do for the ride Womack had to make.
He took the road down Ute Creek, and within half an
hour came to Kelsey's farm.

The marshal was in a field behind the house. When
Womack rode up, Kelsey walked toward him, fat face
wary and suspicious. He said, "Howdy, Womack,"
and waited.

"Slade and his outfit rode into town a while ago,"
Womack said. "Surprised?"

"Not much." Kelsey took a plug of tobacco out of
his pocket and bit off a chew, eyeing Womack as if
uncertain what to expect. "You ride out here to tell me
that?"

"No, but I thought you'd want to know. Might be
trouble, and I hadn't heard you'd resigned your
marshal's job."

"No, I ain't resigned."

"You figure on staying in this country?"

"Sure."

"Then you'd better hit for town."

Suddenly angry, Kelsey flung out, "I'll do my job,
but I sure ain't taking no orders from the likes of you."

"Not orders, Kelsey. Just a suggestion. There's
some changes coming on this range. A man who tries
to keep his feet on both sides of the fence is gonna
have a hell of a rough time."

Kelsey chewed for a moment, then turned and
walked away, calling, "Thanks. I'll go to town."

"I aim to stay here myself, Kelsey," Womack said.
"I'm buying into the Bow and Arrow, and a fence
straddler is one kind of hombre I don't cotton to."

Kelsey wheeled. "All right, all right. I'll get to town right away."

"Have you seen Lud Pierson lately?"

"No."

"Maybe you've seen Mrs. Chapman. Or Abner Lowrie."

It was a long shot, thrown out on the slim chance that Lowrie and Nita had come this way to seek refuge with Molly Pierson or in Owl's Hole; and from Kelsey's panicky expression Womack saw that he had scored.

It took Kelsey a moment to make up his mind. Then he said, in a guarded tone: "No, I ain't seen 'em. Why?"

"Just wondered." Womack thrust back his hat, grinning. "Kelsey, I don't think you'll get to town today. Looks like I'll have to go to Owl's Hole, and I've never been there. I'll pay you to guide me."

"Sorry. Don't know where it is myself."

Womack nodded, as if expecting that. "I'm sorry, too, because I'm going to make this country too hot to hold you. Savvy?"

Emboldened by the knowledge that Womack was going to the Hole, Kelsey shot back: "You don't scare me. You used to, but not now. You'll never get back."

"We'll see," Womack said, and rode on down the creek.

There were a number of farms along the stream, small places in the bottom of a narrow valley that was flanked by frowning red-rock walls. Brown fields lay on both sides of the road. Some held hay still not stacked, others, corn in tall yellow shocks. There were gardens behind every house, the root crops still in the ground.

It was warm in the bottom of the canyon, and the sun beat down upon Womack's back until he finally stopped and tied his sheepskin behind the saddle. This was one part of the country, he thought, that would not be affected by Chapman's ambitions. No matter who survived on the mesa, there would always be a market for the hay and grain and vegetables that were raised there.

It was still early in the afternoon when Womack reined up in front of a shack and called to a farmer who was digging parsnips, "Where's Molly Pierson's place?"

The man straightened, his lips tightly pressed. For a moment he eyed Womack, making no effort to hide his contempt. Then he said sourly, "Next house," and resumed his digging.

Womack rode on, grinning. There was no doubt that this farmer, and probably all the others along the creek, had no love for the Piersons; but he did not fully understand the reason until he reined up in front of a small white cottage and called, "Hello the house."

For a moment there was only silence, but he saw a lace curtain at a front window swing to one side, and he caught a faint blur of a woman's face. The valley was very narrow at this point, with barely enough room for a garden spot behind the house and a long field of grain on down the creek. A small barn stood downstream from the house, a pole corral beside it. The sandstone wall rose directly above the field. It struck Womack that there was not enough farmland here for Molly to make a living.

The door swung open, and a woman came out to stand on the porch. She called in a honey-sweet voice: "Hello. Step down and come in."

Womack hesitated. There was no evidence that anyone else was around, and he had a feeling that if Lud Pierson had decided to hide out until the trouble was over he would not have tarried here. Still, a caution that had more than once saved Womack's life made him ask, "You alone?"

"Of course I'm alone. If I was busy, I'd send you along."

He stepped down and tied as the woman came toward him. She was about thirty-five, he judged, medium tall and very blond. She was heavy with the soft flesh that comes to a woman who leads an inactive life, but she was still physically attractive. Her hair was carefully brushed back and pinned, and her face was bright with rouge.

"Nice day, ain't it?" she asked in the same honey-sweet tone.

"Fine," he said, and walked back to the house with her.

They went in, the woman closing the door. "You'll want a drink, I guess," she said.

Womack glanced around. The room was small and neat, the floor spotless, the wallpaper shocking to the eyes with its startling red pattern. The door into the bedroom was open, and through it Womack could see a bed covered with a white lace spread. He understood now the contempt he had felt in the farmer when he had asked about Molly Pierson's place.

The woman was standing quite close to him. She turned toward a table that held a bottle and some glasses, her ample breasts brushing his arm. He said: "No, I ain't here for a drink. Are you Molly Pierson?"

She swung back to face him, frowning. "Sure I'm Molly Pierson. What in hell did you stop here for if you didn't know who I was?"

"I wanted to be sure. Where's Lud?"

She stepped back, her light-blue eyes wary. "If you ain't here on business—"

"My business, ma'am. Where's Lud?"

"Who are you?"

"Womack."

She sat down in a rocking chair, dropping into it suddenly, as if her knees could not support the weight of her body. She whispered: "Womack! You killed Joe."

She began to rock, her hands folded in front of her, and then she laughed, a dry choking sound that was without mirth. "So you're the great Womack. It's funny, mister, damned funny. You don't look no different than any of a dozen two-bit outlaws who hightail through here looking over their shoulders to see if a posse is breathing down their necks."

"Where's Lud?"

She rose and moved to a back window. "Joe's buried out yonder under that pine tree. Won't he do?"

"No. Where's Lud?"

"I suppose you're fixing to put Lud out there beside Joe?"

"No. I want to take him to town. He's going to do some talking to set a few lies right that he's told."

"I can believe what you said about him lying. He's always been a good liar, Lud has." She faced Womack, breathing hard. "He ain't here, but I can tell you where he is. There's just one thing I want to know. Why didn't you plug him when you got Joe?"

"I didn't have to. He lost his notion about fighting when he saw Joe go down."

"Yeah, Joe was always faster," she breathed. "He was a better man than Lud will ever be, even if Lud always was the one who wore the fine clothes. He's no good, Womack, Lud ain't. I wouldn't be here and I wouldn't be what I am if it wasn't for him. I can't even sell this place and get out because it belongs to Lud. Why, hell, if I had some money, I could go to one of the mining camps and set myself up. A girl does pretty well up there, I hear; but it takes money, and I can't make it here."

"I want Lud," Womack said patiently. "Where is he?"

"He's in Owl's Hole, and you know why? Because he's scared to death of you. He'll wait till the shooting's over and you're gone. Then he'll come crawling out, talking big like always."

The woman's venomous hatred of her brother was startling. Womack rolled a smoke, covertly watching her. He said: "I aim to drag him out. Is he alone?"

She shook her head. "That no-good Lowrie's with him. So's Lowrie's woman. Ain't that a joke, her

coming through here with Lowrie, and him making
me cook a meal for 'em? And her holding her head
high like she was a queen, and all the time she ain't no
different than me. A queen of floozies, that's what she
is." She threw out a hand. "A joke that kills me for
laughing, you hear?"

"I hear," Womack said.

"And her having Cole Chapman for a husband,
with all the things she can get out of him. I'd give ten
years off my life if I could swap places with her, but I
can't. I'm branded just like you're branded. She ain't.
Hell, she could have gone on lording it over everybody; but no, she throws it away for a coyote like
Lowrie. 'Love' she called it." The woman spat the
word at Womack, her face dark with fury. "Yeah, it's a
joke all right."

Womack drew a handful of gold coins from his
pocket and tossed them on the table. "I don't know
how to get to Owl's Hole. Will you guide me for that?"

She stared at the money with greedy intentness.
"That's a hundred dollars, mister. You mean it?"

"I mean it."

"All right, mister. You've made yourself a deal."

Chapter 17: Owl's Hole

WOMACK HAD NOT EXPECTED MOLLY TO TAKE HIS OFFER.
She reached for the gold, but he stepped quickly in
front of her, picked it up, and slipped it into his
pocket. He said: "When we get back. I ain't forgetting
you're Lud's sister."

"You can forget it right now," she flared. "I don't
claim him. I didn't do much crying when we planted
Joe, and I'll do a damned sight less over Lud. You

know something? The only time Slade's wife and the other women on the west end of the mesa ever came to see me was when we buried Joe, and then they couldn't get away fast enough. Respectable they was. Respectable like hell! About like the Chapman hussy."

"You'll get it when we come back," he said.

She frowned, the anger leaving her. "I've heard about you, Womack. They say you're square. Well, I am too. I always give a man what he pays for. If you pay me to take you to Owl's Hole, I'll take you; but you won't come back. They'll shoot you in the back, Lud and Lowrie will."

"I always look out for myself," Womack said.

"Then you'd better look sharp, mighty sharp." She began to unbutton her dress. "If you don't, you won't get back and I won't get paid. Lud will steal everything you've got in your pants and laugh in my face when I say I've got something coming. Wait'll I change."

She went into the bedroom, and taking off her dress, put on a man's shirt and a black riding skirt. She called, "I sure hate to ride, because I'm always sore for three days afterwards, but I reckon there's no help for it."

She came out of the bedroom carrying riding boots, and sat down on the rocker. "My feet swell, too. I reckon a woman can have her dreams, even a woman like me. A hundred dollars will be a start for a nice little house up there in Telluride or Ophir or Rico. I ain't particular." Womack waited while she tugged on a boot, grimacing. She went on: "You take Lud now. I never got nothing from him but the dirty end of the stick. I'm just somebody to cook his meals when he's home and wash his dirty clothes and patch the holes in 'em. Entertain his friends, he says. Well, if that Red Manion was worth two cents, he'd have chased Lud out of the country years ago."

"Things are changing."

"And high time." She pulled on the other boot and rose. "Come on. You can saddle up for me."

She went out through the back, walking awkwardly in her tall heels. He saddled her gray mare and helped her up, then walked around the house to his horse. She rode behind him, a dumpy shape in the saddle, and when he had mounted, she said: "You think I'm a hell of a sister. Well, I'll tell you. He's a hell of a brother. He'd sell me out for a small part of $100."

"You've got to live with yourself," Womack said. "It ain't my worry."

She laughed shortly. "No, it ain't; and as for living with myself, it ain't gonna be hard. Not if I get to where I want to go."

She swung her mare down the trail, and Womack followed. He had never met a woman like Molly Pierson, and he probably never would again. He thought of Nita Chapman, wondering if she had regretted her decision. If she hadn't, she would. She had been trapped by Black Garrity's greed and cupidity; she had turned to Lowrie for the love her husband could not give her, and now there was no escape for her or for Lowrie.

Womack put her out of his mind, his thoughts turning to what lay ahead. If Pierson had been alone in Owl's Hole, the problem would not have been difficult, but the fact that Lowrie was with him put a different face on the matter. Both men were treacherous, and each would gain some courage from the other.

Molly and Womack came to Devil River canyon, where the trail dropped over the rim and reached the bottom in a series of switchbacks. Ute Creek was to their left, running in a white, thundering torrent that finally spilled over a fifty-foot cliff in a lacy waterfall. Molly did not look back as she rode down the trail. She sat her saddle awkwardly, suffering with each jolting step of her mare, but she did not stop until she reached the river. She reined up, and hipping around in her saddle, shook her head at Womack.

"I don't mind going up," Molly said, "but going

down is something I don't like. I keep sliding down on Ivy's neck, and that ain't good for Ivy."

Womack studied the river, wide and slow-moving at this point. He asked, "Swimming water?"

Molly shook her head. "Naw." She pointed to a big cottonwood on the other side, about fifty feet downstream. "Point for that tree and the water won't get up to the belly of your horse. Easiest ford on the river."

Womack glanced at the sun that had swung well over to the west. The snow and cold of the night before seemed a long way off. In this country the altitude largely determined the weather, and he gave a moment's thought to what Rose had said about wintering Bow and Arrow stock at Moran's, and Chapman's ambition to own the valley to the west.

"We'd better ride," Womack said. "How far is it?"

"'Tain't far at all." Molly jerked her head at the north wall of the canyon. "Just over yonder rim. You don't know you're there till you fall into it."

They forded the river, Molly taking the lead, and then angled up the side of the canyon on a trail much like the one they had followed down the other side, red dust rising around them, their mounts laboring and grunting with the climb.

"See the Hole?" Molly asked.

Womack raised himself in his stirrups and looked around. The country to the north rose steadily toward the divide that lay between Devil River and the Uncompahgre. From there the land, covered by a jungle of scrub oak, looked as if it were an unbroken, tilted plain.

He shook his head. "Don't see nothing that looks like a hideout."

"Not many foreigners have seen it except them that are on the dodge," she said. "I get $50 for guiding them in, and I fetch 'em grub when they get low. I charge 'em for that, too, right through the nose. Yes, sir, I reckon there's about five sheriffs on the western slope who'd like to know where Owl's Hole is, but they ain't interested in looking real hard."

She jerked her head and swung to her right. Fifty yards from the rim the Hole opened up before them with surprising suddenness. Screened by the brush so that a man would not see it until he was on the lip of the cliff, the trail wound back and forth to the bottom. They rode down it, the brush tall enough to form a thick cover overhead. Five minutes later they reined up on the level floor of the Hole, Molly saying: "Here you are, mister. It's your worry now." She cocked her head, speculative eyes on him. "Lud ain't gonna cotton to the notion of going with you."

"He'll go," Womack said.

She snorted derisively. "I'd want long odds if I made a bet on you riding out of here."

"I'll pay when I do," he said. "If you want your money, you'd better see I get back."

"Not me, mister," she jeered. "I'll show you where Lud is, but I won't help kill him."

He was silent a moment, listening, but hearing no sound of human presence. From where he sat his saddle he had no idea where he would find Lud Pierson, or how big the Hole was. Apparently it was a long, very narrow canyon with sheer sandstone walls. Above them the slick rock rims projected over the bottom of the Hole so that the sky was no more than a blue ribbon overhead. The sun, Womack thought, would be visible only for a short time near noon each day. It was not a cheerful place.

"Go ahead," she said with cool amusement. "You'll find 'em. Nice spot. Good tight cabin. A spring. Don't get any bad storms down here. Yes, sir, a real nice spot for a man to hide."

He gave her a studying look, wondering if Lud Pierson was somewhere drawing a bead on him this instant. He couldn't trust Molly, not even for $100. He said slowly: "I don't expect to kill Lud, because he won't talk if he's dead, and I aim to make him talk. You could help me do that."

"Nope. It's your show, but I'll give you one piece of advice: leave your horse here and walk in."

It might be a double cross. She could get away with his horse and leave him stranded. Still, there was a good chance she was on the level. She wanted the money, and there was no doubt about the bitterness of her hatred for her brother. If Womack had measured her feeling correctly, she would as soon see her brother dead as not.

He stepped down and left the reins hanging. "You're waiting here?"

"You bet I am. Then I'll ride in and load you on your horse and tote you back to town. I just hope I get there soon enough to grab my $100."

"I don't reckon it'll be me you're toting out of here," Womack said.

Lifting his gun from his holster, he made a quick check and dropped it back. Then he walked warily along the trail, the sense of imminent danger lying like a cold stone in the bottom of his belly.

There was a good chance other men were here besides Pierson and Lowrie. Molly might have lied about that, or she might not have known. If there were, there would be a guard out. Womack understood the kind of men who used hideouts like this; he knew that when they were on the run fear rode with them day and night. That was why the owlhoot trail was dotted with similar hideouts all through the Rockies; and people like the Piersons made a good profit from them. After so many days in the saddle, even the strongest man reached the end of his twine. If he was able to dodge a posse long enough, he invariably made for a hideout like Owl's Hole; but still he was not free from the fear that had become a part of him. The only place where he could sleep would be a refuge that had but one entrance, and that one under constant surveillance.

Stooping, Womack examined the trail. Two horses had passed this way not many hours before. They would be Lowrie's and Nita's. Probably Pierson had been here for some time. Womack went on, wondering how far the clearing was ahead of him.

As soon as he was out of Molly's sight, he ducked off the trail and lay motionless for several minutes, belly down in a mass of dry leaves that had fallen from the scrub oak. He could smell wood smoke now. The cabin, he judged, was not far ahead. Lowrie and Nita, or perhaps all three of them, were having dinner.

Womack crawled forward and stopped, listening. It was warm and dry in the bottom of the Hole. Apparently it had not rained for weeks. The oak leaves crackled with each move that he made, the sound exaggerated to his ears. The clearing was not far ahead of him; he could see the sharper light through a screen of brush. Another ten feet brought him close enough to the edge of the clearing to make out a cabin, a horse shed, and a pole corral.

He pulled his gun, intending to make a run for the cabin that had a blind side toward him. It was then that he heard the sound of a man's running steps behind him, somewhere between him and the bottom of the wall where he had left Molly and the horses.

Chapter 18: The Talking Guns

WOMACK'S FIRST THOUGHT WAS THAT EITHER LOWRIE OR Pierson was behind him, that one of them had been guarding the trail, and that, for some reason, he had not seen Molly and him enter the Hole. He discarded the thought as he stepped into the trail, his gun palmed. In a situation like this, no guard would be that careless. There was one other explanation. The man must not have known Womack, and seeing him with Molly, had made the natural mistake of taking him for a long rider on the dodge who was being guided into the Hole.

The fellow came into view, a stranger to Womack. He was a small man with a knobby face and jumpy black eyes, perhaps someone the Piersons paid to stand guard on the rim whenever a fugitive was in the Hole. The man had a gun in his hand; he took one look at Womack and threw down for a shot.

Womack swore, knowing he was losing any chance he had of surprising Pierson and Lowrie. He fired, knocking the man back on his heels, the guard's bullet snapping over his head through the scrub oak. Again Womack was caught in the old, too-familiar trap. It was kill or be killed, the vicious rule of the shadowy land that lay between the owlhoot and a society controlled by at least some pretense of law.

The guard stopped, jolted by the impact of Womack's slug, left hand involuntarily coming to his side where the bullet had slammed against a rib. He kept his feet and fired again, frantically, in a last desperate attempt to bring his enemy down with him. Womack's second shot caught him in the chest and knocked him down on his belly into the trail.

He was out of the fight, probably dead, but Womack did not take time to find out. Wheeling, he ran across the clearing just as Lud Pierson was going into the cabin with a bucket of water in his hand. Pierson gave out a yell when he saw who it was, and plunged through the door, the bucket banging against one leg and spilling most of the water. Womack reached the east wall of the cabin, breathing hard, thankful that there was no window on this side. For a moment he stood motionless, listening, then he ejected the empty shells and shoved new loads into the cylinder.

He called, "Pierson."

No answer. Again Womack shouted, "Pierson!" Still there was no sound from inside the cabin. Womack, his gun cocked, moved to the front corner. Taking off his Stetson, he hung it on the barrel of his Colt and shoved it forward so that it could be seen from the door. When nothing happened, he put his hat back on his head and took a quick look around the corner. No one was in sight.

"Pierson," Womack called, "I'm taking you to Dogdance. You're gonna tell the truth about what happened at Moran's."

"Womack." It was Nita's voice, so shrill that Womack guessed she was close to hysteria.

"Yeah?"

"Don't come in here after Pierson. I'll get hurt if you do."

"Then send him out with his hands up."

"To hell with you," Pierson bawled. "You'd smoke me down the minute you saw me."

"My word's good," Womack said. "You know that."

"Not when it's my hide you're after. Come in after me if you want me."

Womack hesitated, thinking of Nita. He called, "Nita, you come out."

Silence again, and Womack was certain she had no intention of coming out. Perhaps Lowrie and Pierson wouldn't let her. They would use her as insurance against Womack coming in with his gun smoking. Then he heard a faint sound in the back, a sibilance that might have been made by a boot rubbing on wood. One of them was crawling out through the back window.

"All right, Womack," Pierson shouted. "I'm coming out. Don't shoot. I'm leaving my iron inside."

Womack wheeled and started toward the back, certain that Pierson was lying and that they aimed to catch him in a crossfire between them. It was a move he had not expected; he had thought that neither Pierson nor Lowrie had the courage to face him. He reached the back corner of the cabin just as Lowrie cleared it. They were close to each other, so close that they could not have missed if they had fired instantaneously. For once Lowrie's hawk-nosed face showed surprise. He was visibly shaken. Apparently he had been certain that Pierson's words would hold Womack at the front corner.

Womack reacted instantly. He fired, throwing himself away from the wall. Lowrie took the bullet in his middle, his shot coming a second later and slicing through Womack's coat under his left arm. Womack fell and scrambled up, his gun still lined on Lowrie, who had sprawled headlong and lay still, face down.

Lowrie was out of the fight for good. Womack ran back to the front of the cabin, thinking of all that Nita had given up for Lowrie and what his death would do to her.

"Lowrie, you get him?" Pierson yelled.

As Womack came around to the front of the cabin, he saw Pierson standing just outside the door, gun in his hand, poised, as if uncertain whether to stand or run.

"Throw your iron down," Womack shouted.

Panic struck Pierson then. He brought his gun up, babbling something that did not make sense. Inside the cabin Nita was screaming, a shrill, sustained sound. Womack fired, caught again in a situation where he had no choice. Pierson bent forward, gun dropping from lax fingers. For a moment he swayed, blood making a spreading stain across the front of his silk shirt. Then every joint seemed to give at once, and he fell, his pearl-colored Stetson coming off his head to lie crown down beside him.

Nita was still screaming. Womack holstered his gun, and stepping past Pierson's body, went into the cabin. The woman stood in the middle of the big room, her mouth open, glazed eyes protruding from her head. Womack shook her, saying: "Stop it. Stop it now." He took hold of her and made her sit down. Slowly sanity came back to her, and she began to cry. Womack stood over her, hating Black Garrity and Cole Chapman for what they had done to this woman who possessed so much fire and beauty and love of life, and who, under other circumstances, could have given great happiness to the man she loved.

She felt in her pocket for a handkerchief, found it, and dabbed at her eyes. Then, head bowed, she asked tonelessly, "Abner?"

"He's dead."

"I knew it," she breathed. "You're a devil, Womack. Why couldn't you have let us alone?"

"What'd you expect me to do, stand there and let him plug me?"

She lifted her head to stare at him, dark eyes hating him. "He belonged to me, Womack. Now I have nothing."

"I'll take you back," Womack said. "You can't stay here."

She was silent. She seemed incapable of motion, staring at him, the tears running down her cheeks. Womack turned and went out. Garrity's horse was in the corral. Womack saddled him and brought him to the cabin. Nita was still sitting there, as if she hadn't moved; but when Womack was within a step of her she lifted her right hand from her side. It held a gun. Even then she lacked the will to kill him.

Stepping to her, Womack jerked the gun from her fingers. He said: "Go ahead and cuss me. Hate me all you want to; but someday, when you can think straight, you'll thank me for killing Lowrie. He wasn't good for you, Nita."

"You'll take me back to Dogdance," she said lifelessly. "Cole will—"

"You don't have to go back to him. We'll figure

something out." Womack jerked his head toward the door. "We'd better be riding. Anyone else around here?"

"There was a guard on the rim."

"He won't bother nobody."

Nita rose and walked stiffly toward the door, but Womack stopped her, his right hand making a quick search. She submitted, bringing a hand up to brush across her face, but there was no gun on her.

"I'll always hate you," she said. "You'll never forget what you did today. I'll curse you and I'll hate you."

He thought of the night he had ridden the train out of Denver to Montrose, when he'd dreamed that the ghosts of the men he had killed were jeering and laughing at him. Since he had left the train at Colatas, he had killed four men whose ghosts would join the others. Garrity's words beat against his mind: "You've made your name and you can't get away from it."

"All right," he said roughly, "all right," and pushed her through the door ahead of him.

Nita saw Pierson's body beside the cabin; she stopped, a hand coming up to her throat. She gave a choking gasp and fainted. Womack caught her, thankful that she would not see Lowrie's body. He put her down, carried both bodies into the cabin, and shut the door; then he mounted Garrity's horse, and carrying Nita's limp form in front of him, rode out of the clearing.

The guard lay in the trail where he had fallen. Womack rode around him and returned to the trail. A moment later he came to Molly Pierson, who was standing at the base of the south wall, holding the reins of her mare.

Womack gave her the money, saying: "Your brother and Lowrie are dead. I put 'em inside so the coyotes can't get at 'em, but the guard's still in the trail."

"I'll take care of them," she said stolidly. "Womack, I didn't think you'd pull it off. You must be as good as they say you are."

"Good." He shook his head. "No, I ain't much good. You and me, Molly. Neither one of us."

"I ain't sorry," the woman said quickly. "Lud always used Joe and me to do his dirty work while he took the profit. No, sir, I ain't sorry for Lud. He got what he should have got a long time ago."

"You'll sell your farm and go to some mining camp," Womack said, "but you'll never change."

"Neither will you," she flung at him. "Don't preach to me. From where you're standing, it's out of line."

"I ain't preaching." Womack started to ride on toward his horse, then stopped. "How did we get past the guard?"

"He must have been asleep."

"Looks to me like you were playing both sides."

"I always do," she said coolly. "I called him down after you left."

"Figured he'd get me and you'd save Lud's hide?"

"I didn't care. You and Lud. Not much difference. I always figured a man who lived by the gun oughta die the same way. Fitting and proper."

He stared at the woman's painted face. It showed no trace of regret for the death of her brother. He thought that at least she possessed one virtue: she made no pretense of being anything but what she was. It was his guess she had called the guard down, hoping that the man would kill him and that she could rob his body before Pierson reached it.

"I've got to get Mrs. Chapman to town," he said, "but I'll come back if you want any help."

"I'll get along," Molly said with stony indifference. "The farmers don't like me, but on something of this kind they'll help." She stared at Nita, who had regained consciousness but who still lay motionless in Womack's arms, and she cried out in a sudden burst of fury: "Get her out of here. She's been the cause of all this trouble."

Nita began to tremble. "I'm not. I didn't think it would—"

"Your kind never thinks," Molly screamed. "If it wasn't for you, Joe would be alive."

Womack said, "Shut up," and leading his horse, rode up the trail, Molly still screaming at them. Nita began to cry again, softly.

Chapter 19: A Deal With Nita

IT WAS NOT UNTIL THEY REACHED THE RIVER THAT NITA gained control of herself. She said, "I can ride now."

Womack pulled up and put her down. He dismounted, watching while she knelt in the gravel beside the river and washed her face. The sun was down now, and the light was very thin in the bottom of the canyon. Nita rose and wiped her face with a handkerchief that was already damp with tears. She came toward him, asking in a low voice, "You don't think I'm to blame, do you?"

Looking at her tortured face, Womack could not find the words to tell her that it was exactly what he had thought almost from the first time he had seen her, and that it was what Rose Hovey thought. But they might be wrong. Perhaps it was Black Garrity, or Chapman, or even Grant Hovey, who had been the first on the mesa and had bowed to Chapman's blackmail because he lacked the courage to do anything else.

"No," he said finally. "It isn't that simple. We all make mistakes."

"I made mine when I married Cole," she said bitterly. "Now you're taking me back to him."

He shook his head. "I couldn't do that. What do you want to do?"

"Get out," she said. "Just get out; but I don't have any money."

"You were promising me some the other night."

"I'd have got it from Black," she said. "But he won't give me any to leave with. He'll say I married Cole and I have to go back to him."

"What have you been so anxious to get me out of here for?"

"Abner had it all planned," she said tonelessly. "Slade trusted him, and when the showdown came Abner was going to see that Cole got killed. Then there wouldn't have been any more trouble."

She believed it. He had no doubt of that. He said: "But Lowrie didn't give a damn about what happened to the west-end bunch. He wanted Chapman out of the way so he could put in an irrigation ditch and sell water to the settlers. That it?"

"How did you know? He never talked about it to anyone but me."

"Just a good guess. I'll make a deal with you. Pierson can't tell Slade about Lowrie, so it's up to you."

"No," she cried. "Abner's dead. I couldn't ruin his good name."

"He don't have one," Womack said harshly. "That's where you've been wrong right from the start. Everybody on this range but you figures he killed his father. Slade wouldn't have trusted him if he hadn't been pushed to the place where he was ready to trust anybody who promised to buck Chapman."

She turned away. "I never believed he killed his father."

"You didn't believe it because you were in love with him. No use wrecking your life now because of him. You tell Slade the truth, and I'll see you get out of the country."

She walked to the river and stood there a long moment, then she said: "I can't go back to Cole. As long as I lived, he'd keep reminding me about what I'd done. I tell you I can't go back to him."

"You've got a way out."

Turning, she walked back to him. "All right, I'll tell Slade."

"Ready to ride?"

"I'm ready."

He helped her into the saddle, mounted his own horse, and forded the river, Nita following. They climbed out of the canyon and threaded their way up Ute Creek, the light fading until it was completely dark by the time they reached Jim Kelsey's farm. As they passed the house, Womack saw that the marshal was sitting in the living room, reading. He had not gone back to town, and it was Womack's guess he had not intended to.

There were lights in the saloons and hotel when they reached Dogdance, but except for the horses racked in front of the Belle Union, Main Street was significantly deserted.

They reined up before the Belle Union, Womack saying: "Stay here. I'll fetch Slade."

He stepped down, Nita staring blankly at the front of the saloon. As he walked around the hitch rack and moved across the boardwalk to the batwings, he was not at all sure she would keep her word when the time came to talk. Womack went into the saloon. Slade and Paddy Ryan were standing at the bar talking. The rest of the men were scattered around the room, most of them sitting at tables playing cards. Womack called, "Slade, come here."

The rancher wheeled away from the mahogany, surprised. "So you got back. Me and Ryan was about to make a bet on that. I didn't figure you would."

"Come here," Womack said.

Slade walked to him, Ryan following. There was a moment of silence, the rest of them watching Womack; then they began drifting toward him.

"You talk to Butch?" Womack asked.

"Yep. Talked to Rose Hovey, too. They told the same story. Said the Piersons tried to trick you by pretending they was riding off. Said you got Joe before Lud's gun was out of leather, and he let it go."

"You satisfied?"

"Yeah, I'm satisfied about that, but Lowrie—"

"Come here," Womack said, and went out through the batwings.

Nita had not moved. Womack walked around the hitch rack to stand beside her. He said, "Speak your piece."

She put a hand to the side of her face, shivering, as if the cold breeze flowing down from the mountains penetrated her body. She looked at them, recognized Ryan, and cried, "Paddy, I can't—" She stopped, unable to finish what she had started to say.

"What do you know about Lowrie?" Ryan asked.

"He wanted to get Cole," she said in a low tone. "Nothing else mattered. He had a good dam site and he had the water rights. There was a company in Denver interested in going ahead if he could promise there would be no trouble from the cattlemen."

"Cole would have given him trouble," Ryan prompted. "That it?"

She nodded. "He planned to use Slade and these other men to fight Cole. He was going to kill Cole, and Slade would have got the blame."

They stood there, Slade and the rest, as motionless as a row of stones. Womack turned to them, saying: "Now you know. It don't change nothing except that maybe you can see we're on the same side."

"Yeah, it don't change nothing for a fact," Slade said. "We've still got to fight."

"You can take your men out of town," Womack said. "Chapman's got other fish to fry now, but when he gets around to sending his crew after you I'll see that you hear about it."

Slade scratched his cheek, indecision stamped upon him, then he motioned toward his neighbors. "All right, we'll ride."

Ryan came in long strides to where Womack stood. He said in a low voice: "Chapman and Todd Jarvis are with Garrity in the Starlight. Red Manion and the crew have started the cattle down from Angel Peak, and some of 'em are headed for town."

Womack gave him a thin grin. "Then it'll come."

"We need Slade and his bunch," Ryan argued. "Don't send 'em away."

Womack shook his head. "It'd mean a hell of a fight, and some of 'em would get killed. You and me will do the job. I've got my own debt to settle with Chapman."

"You and me," Ryan cried. "Now look here, Womack, you may be all they say you are, but with odds like that—"

"To hell with the odds." Turning, Womack held up a hand, and Nita stepped down. "Ryan will put the horses up. You stay in your rooms till the stage pulls out in the morning for Colatas. You be on it."

Ryan was shaking his arm. "Use your noggin, boy. There'll never be a better time to settle this than right now when we've got help."

"I told you we'd settle it ourselves," Womack said in a tone that stopped further argument.

Nita started toward the hotel. Womack fell into step with her, and they were halfway across the dust strip when Ryan caught up with them, his voice ragged when he said: "Hovey died this afternoon. Rose and Ed brought the body to town. They're around here somewhere."

Womack stopped. "So that's how Slade had a chance to talk to Rose."

"Yeah, that's right."

Womack remained motionless, wondering if Grant Hovey had regained consciousness before he died. He

said, "I'll take Nita to her rooms, then I'll find Rose
and Ed."

"Ed's on the warpath—" Ryan began, but Womack
went on, hurrying to catch up with Nita.

Chapman would be in one of Nita's rooms,
Womack thought, probably watching as they had
ridden into town, and Garrity was probably with him.

They went into the lobby, which was deserted
except for the clerk, who eyed them with open curiosity. Nita climbed the stairs, Womack behind her,
thinking that if Chapman was here the final settlement was at hand.

When Nita reached the hall, Womack called,
"Wait." She stopped and leaned against the wall,
gripped by a sense of hopeless indifference. Womack
said, "Stay there," and went on to her room. There
was a bracket lamp on the wall at the head of the
stairs, the fringe of its light reaching to Nita's door.
Carefully Womack turned the knob with his left hand,
gun palmed. Chapman's immediate plans would concern Nita, Womack thought. His schemes regarding
Slade and the expansion of the CC would not be
important to him just now, not if the real purpose
behind his scheming had been to impress and hold
Nita. If he had watched the scene in front of the Belle
Union, he would naturally assume that Womack
would come to the hotel with Nita.

Womack pushed the door open and slid in, calling,
"Chapman." There was only the echo of his words in
the empty rooms. He stood motionless, eyes probing
the semidarkness, unable to believe that Chapman
was not there. The shades were up, and a thin light
washed in from the street, but he could not see
anyone.

Nita walked down the hall and came into the room.
She lighted a lamp on the table as Womack said, "Stay
where you are," and went past her into the bedroom.
He had expected a trap; he had nerved himself for it,

and now he felt let down because he had guessed wrong.

Nita shut and locked the front door, then brought the lamp into the bedroom, saying: "No one's here, Womack. What did you expect?"

"Trouble," he said. "I don't savvy. Anybody watching from up here or from the Starlight could have seen us ride into town."

Nita sat down on the bed. She said, "Leave me alone, Womack."

He remained standing there, thinking that she needed help now more than she had ever needed it in her life. He said: "You kept your part of the deal. I'll keep mine."

"In the morning," she said. "The stage doesn't leave till ten."

"Chapman won't wait till morning. He'll show up here and haul you out to the ranch." Womack shook his head. "I thought I had this figured."

"Leave me alone. Just leave me alone."

"I ought to find Rose and Ed, but if I start looking, Chapman will probably come here. I'd better stay in my room. If you need me, holler."

As he turned toward the door, he saw a note on the bureau. He picked it up and glanced at Nita, who was still sitting on the edge of the bed, her eyes on the floor, her face mirroring the abject misery that was in her.

Womack unfolded the note and looked at the bottom. It was signed, "Black." Bringing his eyes back to the top, he read:

The other night Womack told me I had to choose between you and Cole, but I can't quit him. The trouble is, I'm responsible for you coming here, so I owe you something. I left $5,000 in an envelope in Ryan's safe. He'll give it to you in the morning. Take it and leave on the stage if Cole will let you go. It's the best I can do. Don't tell him I gave you *the money. Ryan says Womack has gone after Pierson. If Lowrie's with Pierson, Womack will find you and bring you back; and if he drills Lowrie while he's doing it you'll be lucky.*

Womack put the note back on the bureau. "You'll be all right," he said.

He walked out, leaving her staring at the note. He unlocked the door and stepped into the hall, thinking he should have expected some gesture like this from Garrity. It was the reason the gambler had let him live, but Garrity's note and the money had not solved the problem. If Chapman was alive when the stage left, he would not permit his wife to go. Garrity would certainly be aware of that. As he walked along the hall to his room, Womack wondered what Garrity would do when the moment of final decision came. Probably Garrity didn't know himself, and he was hoping something would happen that would make it possible for Nita to leave without forcing him to break his ties of loyalty to Chapman.

Womack reached his door before he noticed the thin line of lamplight underneath it. He walked on to the head of the stairs, tension building in him again. So that was Chapman's game! He had rigged a trap just as Womack had expected, but it was in his room, not Nita's.

For a moment Womack remained at the head of the stairs, then he catfooted back to his door and drew his gun. Slowly he turned the knob, then shoved the door open and plunged in. He stood motionless, feeling foolish and knowing he was jumpy. He should not have expected Chapman or any of his men to be there. There would not have been a light in the room if they had been.

Rose was sitting in a chair beside the window, and he saw at once that she had been crying. Now she got up and came to him, trying to smile. She said: "I've been praying you'd come here, Bill. I've been terribly afraid I'd miss you, but I didn't know where else to wait."

He took her hands. "Ryan told me about your dad. I'm sorry—"

"No, Bill. It isn't that. Dad never regained consciousness. He just quit breathing. It's all right. He's happier now, I think. He's never been happy since he got here. Or after Chapman came, anyhow." She saw he did not understand, and went on: "I'm not afraid of death, and I'm not afraid of it for Dad. Not if the Lord is the kind of God I've always pictured Him."

"I hoped your dad would be able to tell you and Ed—"

"That's the trouble," she broke in. "He couldn't, and Garrity got hold of Ed and convinced him that you shot Dad. Now Ed says he'll kill you."

"He couldn't believe that. He's smart enough to see what Garrity's up to."

"But he does believe it. Garrity has a reputation for integrity, but it's more than that. You see, I told Ed about you wanting to buy in with us, and somewhere Garrity had heard the same thing."

"I told him."

"I didn't know, but it isn't important. You see, Ed never believed Dad went to the CC to jump Chapman. He thinks—and it's what Garrity has made him think—that you shot Dad in the back when he was coming home because you wanted us to inherit the Bow and Arrow and you knew Dad wouldn't stand for you buying into the ranch."

He saw how it fitted together, how Garrity in his sly way had done a perfect job of twisting the facts. "But Ed can't fight me. What does he know about a gun?"

"Nothing," she breathed. "He knows you'll kill him if it comes to a fight, but it's something he can't get away from. We've always thought Dad was a coward. It didn't make much difference to me, but it has to Ed. It's been a shadow over his life ever since he's been old

enough to notice things like that. Garrity knows how
it's been. He's so terribly shrewd. He's made Ed think
he has to fight you to prove he isn't a coward like
Dad's been."

It came to him then, the full implication, and all
that it meant to him and Rose. He had never run out
on a fight with anyone. The pride that had grown in
him through the years would not let him run now, but
if he killed Rose's brother he could not hope to have
her love.

He walked past her and sat down on the bed, hand
automatically moving to his pocket for the makings.
He knew that Garrity had been trapped by conflicting
ties of loyalty, and he had caught Womack in the same
kind of trap. It seemed to Womack that the end of the
world had come. He had caught a brief glimpse of
Heaven, and then the door had been slammed in his
face.

Chapter 20: Gunman's Pride

FOR A LONG TIME WOMACK SAT MOTIONLESS ON THE EDGE
of the bed, the sack of Durham and package of papers
in his hand, while the bitterness of disappointment
and frustration corroded his soul. Love! He had never
known what it was before; he had even felt a little
contemptuous of a man who did foolish things for a
woman.

To Bill Womack it had always been a simple proposition. The world was filled with women. Some, like
Molly Pierson, could be bought for a few dollars.
Others, like Nita Chapman, could be bought for a
greater price. He raised his eyes to Rose; he saw the

brown freckles on her nose, her auburn hair and the small rebellious curl that lay along her forehead, her dark blue eyes that were filled with worry. Rose Hovey could not be bought. Not for any price. He had felt a deep, unswerving honesty in her from the first moment he had met her in Colatas. It seemed a long time ago. Much had happened in a few hours; no more, perhaps, than had happened in a similar span of time before in his life, but it meant more. His future. And Rose's. And Ed Hovey's.

He shook some tobacco into a paper, rolled the cigarette and sealed it, his mind turning back to the first time he had met Ed in the Denver hotel. A good kid, he had thought, still half boy, who looked as if he'd sprouted up out of his boots. Womack remembered that he had been envious. He'd have swapped places with Ed if he could; if he'd been able to live his life over he'd have liked to have started the way Ed had. Now the kid was bent on throwing it away. No good. There wasn't anything good about it. He fired the cigarette, pulling his eyes away from Rose and thinking of Garrity's words, "You've made your name, and you can't get away from it," words that built a wall separating him from Rose. There wasn't anything he could do for Ed. That was the hell of it. He knew how it was because he had gone through the same thing. Ed had to do it. Garrity, who knew human nature so well, had played on Ed's pride and shame the way a master plays on a violin.

Garrity and Chapman knew that Ed would go down before Womack's gun if they fought. Perhaps they planned to set a trap and gun Womack in the back before he got Ed. Or perhaps they'd let Ed die, knowing that Womack would not stay on Dillon Mesa after that. Either way, it accounted for the fact that there had been no trap in Nita's room. Garrity had thought of something better.

Womack had no sense of time. He sat there, hunched forward, the cigarette cold between his lips.

Rose came to him, asking in a low tone, "What are you going to do, Bill?"

"I can't run," he said, staring at the floor. "I can't run any more than you and Ed could have let your dad sell out to Chapman. It just ain't in me."

"But he's only a boy."

"He's as old as you, and you're a woman."

"Just in years, Bill."

"You said you two thought alike."

"We always have, but this is different. He wants to be a man. He thinks he's got to live down Dad's reputation. If he could be convinced that Dad went to the CC to jump Chapman, it would change everything."

Womack knew it was true. Ed could have pride in his father's memory instead of shame, but there was no way to convince him. Chapman and Garrity would not tell the truth, and Jarvis, who had shot Grant Hovey in the back, would not talk. Nita hadn't actually seen the shooting, so there was no one Ed would believe who would tell him how it had been. If Ed had time to think it over, he would finally see what Garrity was doing; but there was no time. Ed was waiting for Womack, probably in the Starlight. If he didn't show up there, Ed would come here. Again Womack found himself in the old familiar situation: kill or be killed. But there was one difference. He couldn't kill Ed. If he let Ed kill him, he would not be helping the boy. Sooner or later young Hovey would learn the truth, and Womack's death would be a burden on his conscience as long as he lived.

"What are you going to do?" Rose asked again.

"What do you want me to do?"

"Leave town," she whispered. "This isn't just running, Bill. I thought you—I mean, we—" She ran a tongue over dry lips. "I'm not much, Bill, but I'll go away with you. We'll leave Ed here, and he can have the ranch. We'll go to South Park and buy that place you like."

He got up and looked down at her upturned face. "I love you," he said slowly. "I love you so much I don't want you that way."

She walked away from him and stood by the window, staring down into the darkness. "I love you, too, Bill."

He stared at her back, the sweat breaking out on his face. He wanted her and he could have her. They could sneak out through the back and go down the alley to the livery stable. They could get horses and ride away. For a moment temptation sang a sweet siren song in his ears, and then it faded. The story would follow him. He'd seen it happen to other men. They'd say Bill Womack had lost his guts. He'd backed down and run from a kid who had never killed a man in his life. No, he couldn't do it. Not even for Rose. Pride, just foolish pride, but Womack had followed his trade too long to break it down.

It came to him, the knowledge shocking him, that Rose Hovey could be bought. Her brother's life was the price. Only her love for Ed could bring her to a decision like this, the kind of love that had never been in Bill Womack's life. He came to her and put his arms around her. She stood that way for a long moment, still staring into the darkness, the back of her head against his chest.

"It wouldn't work," he said at last. "After a while you'd hate me, and maybe I'd hate you for making me run."

"No, it wouldn't work." She took a ragged breath that was almost a sob. "I think I know what hell is, Bill. It must be choosing between two men you love."

He was silent for a time, a plan taking shape in his head. It was not a good plan. He had hoped to stay here until Chapman and Garrity came for Nita, and when they did he would force the settlement with them in his own way and at a time of his own choosing. Now he could not do that. They wouldn't come, for they would be counting on Garrity's lies doing the job for them.

"Maybe there's a way out of this," Womack said. "Will you trust me?"

"I'd trust you for anything," she whispered.

"I'm not sure it'll work, but it'll be better than waiting. You go to the Starlight and get Ed. Tell him I'm in my room. Tell him anything. Just get him out of there."

"Maybe he isn't in the Starlight."

"I've got a hunch he is. If he ain't, see that he don't come in. Will you do that?"

"I'll try."

"Give me five minutes," Womack said, and turning, walked out of the room and down the hall to the back stairs.

He paused there in the fringe of light from the wall lamp, checked his gun, and dropped it back so that it rode loosely in his holster. Then he went down the stairs and out of the back door into the alley. When he came to the rear of the Starlight, he saw that a man was working on the loading platform, a lantern hung from a nail in the wall above a row of beer barrels.

Casually, Womack asked, "Garrity inside?"

The man straightened, looking curiously at Womack. "Yeah, he's in there. So's Chapman and Todd Jarvis. The Hovey kid, too. Lot of talk about some shooting. You'd better stay out of there, mister."

"I just want to see Garrity for a minute," Womack said, stepping up on the platform.

Suspicious now, the man said, "Ain't no time to go visiting, mister."

"I ain't visiting," Womack said irritably. "Garrity owes me something, and this is a good time to collect."

Womack pushed past the man into the storeroom; he shut the back door and threw the bolt. The man heard it and began to kick on the door, cursing him in

an angry voice. Womack went on, ignoring him, and
threaded his way through the darkness to the door
that opened into the saloon. Womack paused, listening. He could hear voices, but they were from the
front of the saloon, too far away to identify. He
opened the door a crack. Still he could not see the
length of the room, and he was not sure who was
there; but his five minutes were almost gone, he knew,
and he had no more capacity for waiting. He shoved
the door open another foot and slid into the saloon.

Chapman and Jarvis were standing in the front of
the room, Chapman beside the bar, Jarvis some
distance to his left. Garrity was behind the mahogany,
and in that one quick glance Womack saw that the
regular bartender was not there. Ed Hovey was no-
where in sight. Womack walked toward them, his
mind working with sharp clarity as he took in the
situation. The job had to be done now, quickly, before
Ed returned. Rose would not be able to hold him away
for more than a few minutes.

It was Jarvis who saw Womack first. He swore,
shouting, "The gunslick."

Chapman wheeled, peering through his glasses at
Womack. Garrity called: "I guess you want Ed Hovey,
Womack. You must have heard he was looking for
you."

Womack ignored it. There was just one thing that
would open this up, and it had to be opened at once,
or Garrity would play it along until Ed came back.

"I killed Abner Lowrie today, Chapman," Womack
said in a hard voice. "He should have been your meat.
If I was married to a woman and she ran off with
another man, I'd want to kill that man."

"Get out of here," Garrity shouted. "Damn you,
Womack, Ed Hovey's looking for you. If you're half
the man you're supposed to be—"

"Shut up." Womack came on, walking slowly and
keeping Garrity in the range of his vision. "I'll tell you
something else, Chapman. Your wife's in the hotel,

and she's leaving town on the stage in the morning. I don't usually mix in family business, but I'm mixing in this. I aim to see she gets out of town."

It was the only thing Womack could have said that was strong enough to make Chapman pull his gun. He gave out a strangled, incoherent cry and started to run along the bar, right hand clawing for his gun. Womack drew and threw his first shot at Garrity, judging him to be the fastest of the three. He got Garrity in the right arm, the impact of the heavy slug knocking the gambler half around.

Chapman had his gun out now; he leveled it and fired, but his glasses did not entirely correct his nearsightedness, and he missed. Womack caught the blur of Todd Jarvis's hand sweeping gun from leather, and he knew he must make a choice. Without Chapman, Jarvis would be nothing. Chapman was still running in his awkward way, left foot swinging out, and he had time to get in one more shot before Womack whipped his gun to him and cut him down.

Womack expected Jarvis to be in the fight before this. He heard a shot from the batwings and swung a glance that way as Chapman fell. Paddy Ryan was standing there with a smoking .45 in his hand while Jarvis was spilling forward on his face.

Chapman had lost his gun. Now he brought himself to his hands and knees and reached for it, but his strength was flowing out of him in a red tide. He fell back to the floor, blood bubbling at the corners of his mouth, and he died that way, the clutching fingers of his hand a few inches short of the gun.

Womack lined his gun on Garrity and moved to the bar. It was then that the batwings burst open and Ed Hovey plunged in, his face white. He shouted, "Womack, I'm going to—"

"Shut up." Ryan jammed a gun into his back. "You're just a wet-eared kid trying to be a man. Shut up now and listen."

Womack kept his eyes on Garrity. The gambler's

right arm hung grotesquely at his side, his dark face rigid as he fought the agony that swept through him. Womack asked, "How good are you with your left, Garrity?"

"No good at all," Garrity said. "I had a hunch the first time I saw you that you were going to be bad medicine. I wish to hell Lowrie had drilled you that night."

"I was watching outside, expecting something like this," Ryan crowed. "Never seen a faster draw, and I've seen a lot of 'em. You'll do with the best, Womack."

Ed stood motionless, eyes leaping from Jarvis's body to Chapman's and then to Womack. He called out: "I'll get you, Womack. You ain't changed nothing by plugging 'em."

"Garrity's gonna change things," Womack said quietly. "I never have killed a man who couldn't pull, but I will now if he don't talk."

"I figure to live a long time." Garrity looked at Chapman's body, shaking his head. "He was quite a man, Womack, in some ways. He had two talents. One was making money and the other was getting men to work with him; but when the chips were down I wasn't good enough, and he was counting on me."

"You gonna talk—"

"No sense not to, now." Garrity's lips tightened as he put his left hand against the bar to steady himself. "We made a fool out of you, Ed. Todd Jarvis shot your dad after he left the CC. Grant rode over to tell Cole he was quitting the combine. He cussed Cole out good, but Cole wouldn't fight."

Ed raised a hand to his forehead, trembling like a scared kid. It would be all right with him now, Womack thought. He said, "Maybe you'll live a long time, Garrity—somewhere else."

"Sure," Garrity breathed. "I'll take the stage with Nita when she goes. I'll sell the Starlight to you, Ryan.

Cheap. You're the nearest thing to a doctor in this burg. Fix my arm."

Turning, Womack walked out. He crossed the store-room and threw the bar on the back door. When he reached the loading platform, he saw that the man who had been working there was gone. He vaulted into the alley and began to run toward the livery stable.

He couldn't stay here. He loved Rose too much to stay and not marry her, and he couldn't marry her. No matter how she felt toward him, she'd get over it in time. Time! That was the answer to all of this. She'd find some other man. She'd forget him.

He came into the stable from the alley. Seeing the liveryman at the other end of the runway, he shouted: "I want to buy the horse I had today. The saddle, too. How much?"

The liveryman stood in the cone of light thrown by a lantern hanging overhead. He stared at Womack, catching the urgency that was in his voice, and he said slowly, "Well now, he's a good animal—"

"How much?"

"Why, I guess $100—"

"All right, all right," Womack said, and gave him the money.

He had the blanket on the horse and was reaching for the saddle when he heard Rose say, "Bill, you aren't leaving?"

He swung toward her, swearing softly. He had hoped to get out of town without seeing her. It would have been easier. He said, "Yeah, I'm sloping out."

She came toward him, head held high. She asked, "Ed?"

"No. Garrity told him."

"Then why?"

He swallowed, fighting a desire to take her into his arms. He said: "Garrity told me once that I'd made my name and I couldn't get away from it. He said I'd wind up with some trigger-happy kid's slug in me. I couldn't drag you through that, Rose. I've got the mark on me, and I'll never get it off."

She stood close to him, the lantern light falling full upon her face. She said: "Bill, I know what's in your mind, and I love you for it, but there's one thing you haven't thought of. Everybody on Dillon Mesa needs you. There's a lot of work to be done."

He stared at her hungrily, wanting to stay more than he had ever wanted to do anything. She must have sensed his feelings, for she hurried on: "There's no evil in the talent you have for using a gun. The evil or the good comes in the way a talent is used. And Bill, if you're killed by some glory-hunting kid, I'll be thankful for whatever time I've had with you."

He turned toward the saddle, then he felt her hand on his arm. She was right about the mesa people needing him: Kelsey, who was a disgrace to the star that he wore; Red Manion, who might be a good sheriff now that Chapman was gone; the barber, just wanting a chance to make a living for his wife and his kids; Slade, and his neighbors who would be reaching for better graze; Ed, who would be needing an older man's guidance.

"Bill," Rose said, "look me in the face. Tell me you don't love me."

"I can't do that," he said.

"Then I'm going with you."

He dropped his hands from the saddle; he looked at her, and it came to him that he had been about to do the wrong thing. It was not too late to change, not too late at all.

He kissed her, and her arms came up around his neck, and her lips were sweet and clinging. This was the way he had known it would be if he ever kissed her. He could never leave her now.

REAL WEST

The true life adventures of America's greatest frontiersmen.

THE LIFE OF KIT CARSON by John S.C. Abbott. Christopher "Kit" Carson could shoot a man at twenty paces, trap and hunt better than the most skilled Indian, and follow any trail — even in the dead of winter. His courage and strength as an Indian fighter earned him the rank of brigadier general of the U.S. Army. This is the true story of his remarkable life.

__2968-5 $2.95

THE LIFE OF BUFFALO BILL by William Cody. Strong, proud and courageous, Buffalo Bill Cody helped shape the history of the United States. Told in his own words, the real story of his life and adventures on the untamed frontier is as wild and unforgettable as any tall tale ever written about him.

__2981-2 $2.95